MOONCALFS

DAVID O'BOYLE

268 Kensington Avenue

Bayport, NY 11705

doboyled@gmail.com

Printed in the United States of America

 Created with Vellum

For mom and dad.
And for anyone who ever needs a friend.

Contents

A Cook or a Grave Digger

Cameron's stomach had been upset since the night before. Despite that fact, he still felt like taking his morning jog. A seemingly satisfactory decision at first, it was fast becoming clear that he should have stayed home.

In distress, he thought to himself, *If I can just make it down the Old Shoaling Road, I'll be okay.*

That logic was based upon the geography of the road in question. After it meandered alongside a canal for nearly a mile, the Old Shoaling Road descended upon a little town beach overlooking the bay. Cameron recalled that this little town beach contained a little beach parking lot. More importantly, situated in between this little beach and this little beach parking lot was a maintenance shed with a restroom.

Sadly, when Cameron reached the maintenance shed, the restroom was locked. A sign on the door posted the hours of operation. Cameron didn't know the time. All he knew was that if the restroom wasn't open now, it didn't matter when it would be.

A brief scan of his surroundings brought his attention to the other end of the parking lot, where, in the thick of an abandoned construction site, there was a porta-potty. His feet took him in that direction as a result. They did not get far before Cameron realized he needed another alternative. Chains were wrapped around the door handle of the porta-potty. Entry was impossible.

Panicked and out of civilized options, Cameron had no choice but to cart his bowels towards Mother Nature's nearest bathroom.

With a straight sprint and some sound clenching, there was a chance he could reach a thicket of cattails and shrubbery in time.

Nope. He was unable to hold it.

His underwear was finished. If he hurried, perhaps he could salvage his shorts.

Another unexpected squirt ruined that possibility. Brown streamed down his upper thighs and calves, overpowered the garrison that was his leg hair, and puddled in the rim of his socks. When he reached the cove, he jumped in the shrubbery and pulled down his shorts to push out the leftovers.

A hand tapped him on the shoulder. "Find another bush."

"I'm sorry, sir, it was an emergency, I had no choice," Cameron said.

"Officer," the voice said to correct him on his proper title. Cameron groaned at the thought of dealing with one of 'those' types of cops. "Now, turn and face me, and show some respect," the voice said with an angrier tone.

Cameron complied without question.

The person standing behind him was a woman who was dressed like a homeless person.

"Scare ya?" the homeless-looking woman said. "Didn't

mean to. Though it looks like someone already did," she said, pointing to the feces running down Cameron's leg.

"The ideal man bears the accidents of life with dignity and grace," Cameron said.

"I see someone's read some philosophy. Aristotle also said that all knowledge must begin with information from the senses, which isn't good for us because our noses are full of shit," the homeless-looking woman said.

"I thought you were...," Cameron said.

"Career-military?" the homeless-looking woman said. "Desert Storm? Operation Iraqi Freedom? Because I'm all of those things."

"Go figure," Cameron said.

"Here's something to go figure...shave your face," the homeless-looking woman said.

"Rocking a little peach fuzz is in right now," Cameron said.

The homeless-looking woman went over and grabbed his cheeks with her right hand. "What are you hiding under there," she yelled.

"A face that could launch a thousand ships," Cameron said.

"What do you know about war and what launches ships? You've never worn the uniform," the homeless-looking woman said as she released his face.

"No, but I once considered it," Cameron said.

"I'm not talking little kid fantasies with sticks and cap guns. You'd never actually enlist," the homeless-looking woman said.

"Probably not. But don't act like you know my life," Cameron said, even though it sounded like she did.

Cameron detested war. He considered it an antiquated method of conflict that should have gone out of style with the Stone Age. Even so, he questioned whether other factors influenced his decision not to enlist. To him, there seemed to be no denying that inside all men is an inner Achilles, a subliminal yearning to pursue a warrior's life and be hailed a hero. For this reason, it was hard to view cadets in cotton whites or marines in navy blues without a degree of envy. Regardless of how many books he read on the subject, in a single tour, they saw the world in a way Cameron never could. That sense of missing out disappointed him. In fact, not only did it disappoint him, it was fast becoming the prevailing motif of his life. Other people went off and lived their lives. Cameron just sat at home and wondered what if.

"I'm sorry. I didn't mean to be so blunt. Let me make it up to you. Follow me," the homeless-looking woman said.

Cameron trailed her into the brush to an old wooden bench overlooking a cove. From decades of flood and storm, a type of fossilization had taken place around the bench's metal legs, specifically where they formed into feet. Yet despite these evident examples of age, it was another feature of the bench that made the best claim for its case as a relic. A totem to young romance, a set of initials had been carved into the wood amidst the hearts and arrows of temporary teenage love.

The homeless-looking woman took a seat and stretched her legs to catch the first rays of sunlight. Her pants were trimmed to the length of shorts and hiked up towards her groin. As she extended herself further and further, it became clear that her odd maneuvering had a purpose besides comfort. A flask lay adjacent to the other side of the rock. The homeless-looking woman grabbed it and unscrewed the top, thereby emanating quite a strong smell.

"Care for a nip?" the homeless-looking woman said.

Normally, Cameron would hesitate before taking a swig from a stranger's flask, especially when that stranger was a stranger he met in the woods while taking a shit, but Cameron was so disgruntled with life lately that things which earlier appeared to be poor choices now seemed worthy of some second guessing. Who knew, maybe some extra risks here and there could be a good thing?

As soon as the booze hit his lips, he grimaced so hard that his cheeks swallowed his eyes. Fire water coated his throat with such a ferocity he felt his esophagus could melt. While this went on, he desperately tried to keep down his vomit, an act that was a vestige behavior of his college days, when doing so was how one saved face. A flower-curdling burp, therefore, replaced the puke.

"It's good. Hurts at first. Then it feels nice," Cameron said.

"Agreed," the homeless-looking woman said, signaling for the flask. When she got it back, she took a swig with minimal effort. Then she handed it back to Cameron. Peer pressure and pride made him replicate her actions.

Again, the stinging sensation overtook him when the liquor attacked his throat.

He puked.

Vomit went everywhere.

The homeless-looking woman laughed hysterically.

"You should've seen your face. The Viet Cong didn't squint that much when staring at the sky looking for aircraft," the homeless-looking woman said as she took another swig and wiped the liquid from the sides of her mouth. Cameron sat next to her on the bench to clear the chunks of vomit from his shirt and regroup from what had just happened. The day was only an hour old, and he was already exhausted. This pleased him, even if the exhaustion was mostly the result of oral and rectal excretion. It diminished the anxiety he would feel later in the day to get something accomplished.

"You see that up there?" the homeless-looking woman asked. Her head was raised to the sky.

Above them, a hawk perched on a narrow branch above the cove. After it peered over at the two of them, it darted into the sky, circling higher and higher above the cove until it was cradled in the clouds, rocking back and forth on the winds like boats on the water.

"Poetry in motion," the homeless-looking woman said while taking another drink.

"Lord of the sky," Cameron said.

With that, the homeless-looking woman rose from her seat on the bench and pretended to aim at the bird, closing one eye and acting like she had a gun on her shoulder. "You'd be surprised how fast the infallible can fall...for a shot like this, I'd adhere to Viet Kong tactics. Learn to recognize the sound, speed, and silhouette of the target. Improve your calculations. Figure out how far in front of the nose you need to aim when it dives or when it's flying flat. When their northern villages were being pounded by U.S. air strikes, they all learned the techniques. Warriors. Women. Children. The whole lot of 'em."

"What good would any of that do for the Viet Cong without the right weapons?" Cameron said.

The homeless-looking woman shook her head and offered a half-smile. "You'd be surprised. The most dangerous job in Vietnam for U.S. servicemen was flying helicopter missions. We lost 4,869 birds that way during that damned war."

"A philosopher and a historian," Cameron said.

"The military has its down time. I used it to catch up on my reading. 'Nam in particular caught my interest, especially the helicopters. I loved learning about the helicopters. I fancy anything big with an engine."

"I wouldn't have expected that," Cameron said.

"Because a woman can't be the engineering type?" she asked him.

"Look" Cameron said, trying to change the subject from that uncomfortable exchange.

The hawk plunged down in free fall, increasing its speed every second before it crashed against the water and vanished. Out of the middle of the ripples, the bird emerged and skyrocketed upward, this time with company. Clamped inside its talons was a squirming black eel that was making one final attempt to escape nature's finest pair of vice grips. But to no avail. Before long, the aerial ensemble concluded. What followed was a slimy snack for a Lord of the Sky.

"As a veteran, what are your views on the current wars we're in?" Cameron asked.

"Evil is not just evil for the sake of being evil. Beyond that, all I'll say is that the world is stuck in the mud in certain places," the homeless-looking woman said.

"Just like our toes," said Cameron.

"Indeed," the homeless-looking woman said, more interested in fiddling with the bright orange seafaring rope curled up on the ground next to her side of the bench than talking any more about war.

"What's the rope for?" Cameron asked. He felt that a sudden deep gloom had taken over the homeless-looking woman. Since he was familiar with those types of sensations, he wanted to help her. The best way he knew how was by maintaining conversation.

"I usually use it to anchor my pink polka dotted kayak. You see it over there in those bushes. But today I'm thinking about using it to hang myself," she said.

"Why's that?" Cameron asked.

"I recently transitioned. It did not go over well. My mother recently passed, and I think I'll be blamed," she said.

"Well, did you do it? Did you kill her?" Cameron asked.

There was a brief silence.

"No, I didn't," the homeless-looking woman said.

"You didn't what?" Cameron asked.

"No, I didn't kill my mother," the homeless-looking woman yelled at him.

There was another brief silence. Then the homeless-looking woman burst out laughing. So did Cameron.

"Sometimes you just have to say things out loud to realize their absurdity," Cameron said.

"What are you, a therapist?" the homeless-looking woman asked.

"No...a patient," Cameron said.

The homeless-looking woman laughed again.

"I've seen a lot of therapists. And none of their advice has ever been more effective than the power of a good laugh. Thank you for that," she said. "I can't tell you how much that means. How can I return the favor?"

"I don't know. Any thoughts on what I should do with my life?" Cameron asked.

"My father told me once that people are always going to eat and die. So, he suggested becoming a cook or a grave digger."

"Yet you became a soldier?" Cameron asked.

"I didn't give a shit what my father wanted me to do," the homeless-looking woman said.

"As interesting as your daddy issues sound, if you'll excuse me, I'm just going to jump in and rinse these clothes off in the cove."

"Shoes and all?" the homeless-looking woman said.

"Shoes and all," Cameron said.

"As fun as that sounds to watch, I should be going," the homeless-looking woman said.

"Where to?" Cameron asked.

"I'm dropping this kayak off with a friend," the homeless-looking woman said.

With that, she paddled off in her pink polka dotted kayak up the canal and out of sight.

2

An Infamous Shack Just Outside Drumcliffe

After a careful weighing of his options, Cameron decided it best to put his shirt back on. Salty and wet as it was, discomfort defeated sunburn. Plus, the raggedy white tee went well with his raggedy shorts, whose pocket-less nature created an inability to carry a cell phone, money, or anything else of value to help him get back home. Why such an incompetent design of pocket-less shorts ever made it past the prototype was beyond him, and it was even more beyond him how he had so many different pairs of these same shorts to promote the continuance of their production.

When the clothing predicament was resolved and he was dressed, Cameron contemplated the options available for his soaking wet footwear. Since his socks were beyond repair, the solution for them would be in the bottom of a trash can, when he found one. On the contrary, if allowed time to dry, his shoes seemed salvageable. Based on this belief, Cameron tossed the shoes in a tree beside the road where they could aerate in the breeze. They hung low enough on a branch so Cameron could easily retrieve them when he so desired.

Just as he started to look for a trash can for his socks, an old man approached him. "Young man, young man," the old man said. The old man wore an aged flat cap on his head that had seen better days. To complement the cap, he sported a white button-down shirt. This was tucked into black slacks that were pulled up alarmingly close to his nipples. His loafers, the only thing that didn't match the suit other than the flat cap, were brown and worn from walking.

"Quite the predicament you have there, young man," the old man said, referring to the shoes in the tree. When the old man smiled, he revealed a gleaming set of white teeth. Even if they were false, Cameron was pissed that the geezer had better chops than him.

"Oh, it's no big deal. I put them up there to dry," Cameron said.

"It's a good day for such a thing, I suppose. Great breeze. Beautiful weather," the old man said. "Reminds me of where I grew up."

"Where's that?" Cameron asked. He figured it was better to be respectful and voluntarily continue the conversation if the old man was going to keep talking either way.

"Across the pond, as they say. Ever been?" the old man asked.

"Nope, haven't had the chance," Cameron said, though he knew that was a lie. He could've gone just as easily as anyone else in upper-middle-class suburbia. The reason why he didn't go was that he was afraid; afraid of being away, afraid of being stranded in a place where, if all went wrong, he couldn't just hop on a bus and get home. That home base, that safety within an automobile's grasp, was his constant comfort. Any area outside of that zone made him panicky. The what-if demons ran through his mind conjuring up doomsday scenarios. What if I'm alone? What if I go crazy? What if I lose my mind? What if it gets so bad that...that...I end it? He shuddered at this thought, captured it, and returned it to the recesses of his mind. At first, he felt guilty for having the thought. Then he felt guilty for being so hard on himself for something not entirely within his control.

He took a deep breath and remembered his mindfulness techniques; he let the air enter his nose and filter out again. He allowed himself to remember what was good and real and what was wrong and imaginary. Some positive self-talk came next. With as much compassion as he could muster, he assured himself that even though life was hard, it would get better when he found a girl, figured out his purpose, stopped trying to be perfect at everything, and embraced the future as a friend and not a foe.

Of course, no such answer was presented to the old man. If he mentioned anything like those ruminations, he would look weak. So, he said this instead: "I didn't go because I thought it was stupid. What can you really learn about a country as a semi-permanent tourist? All your time is spent with other Americans, and when you actually see the city, you see it from tourist traps. It's the same thing when people visit New York City. They visit the Empire State Building, they see Times Square, they see a play...within a week, they're saying Fughettaboutit, and they've never even been to Brooklyn."

"I only ask because we were talking about the weather, and in Europe, there are two ways to answer questions about the weather," the old man said.

"What's that?" Cameron asked.

"The English way and the German way," the old man said.

"In England, if you talk to a stranger about the weather, they get excited at the prospects of conversation. In Germany, on the other hand, they get offended. They find it trivial."

"Is that why they fought each other in two world wars?" Cameron asked. "All that miscommunication?"

"The most difficult questions sometimes have the simplest answers...but who knows?" the old man said as he removed his cap and wiped the sweat from his brow. When that was done, he polished his forehead with some sunblock and caked everything leftover onto his nose. While he continued applying, he informed Cameron of the importance of fair-skinned people protecting their skin. Then he handed Cameron the bottle.

"It isn't realistic for me to take preventative measures for melanoma twenty years before I get it," Cameron said. "I could be dead tomorrow. I don't want to spend all of my time investing in the future."

"I remember when Coppertone bought sunscreen and they unleashed that brilliant marketing campaign in the 50-60's with the little girl and the dog pulling at her underwear," the old man said. Then he explained how the product developed in the 40's when American GI's were burning up in the Pacific and needed some type of skin protection. "My wife got hooked on it because she loved the sun. I've heavily applied it ever since she showed it to me."

"How's that worked out for you?" Cameron said.

"In the early 90's, I had melanoma," the old man said.

"So, it didn't help," Cameron said.

"It kept me from getting it in the 80's. You have to understand something when it comes to life, young man. It's one thing to live life without regrets, it's another thing to be just plain stupid. It's a quick squeeze out of a bottle. What are you doing with your life that you can't spare a second for that?" the old man asked.

"I'm trying to figure that out," Cameron said.

"Well, just be happy you live in a time and place where you have the liberty of that dilemma," the old man said. "I sure as hell didn't. By the looks of you, your folks probably didn't either. Whereabouts is your family from?"

"Sligo County, Ireland," Cameron said.

"Ah, wonderful country," the old man said. "Sligo has the only mountains in the country that rival Galway. Fine people up there. And great food, too. The best food, actually." And with that, the old man started his story without worrying whether Cameron cared to hear it. It went something like this:

On the outskirts of Drumcliffe, in a town in Connacht Province, Sligo County, Ireland, there was a road that slithered down to the bay. Generations of fishermen spent their lifetimes lugging their catch to market over its unforgiving surface. In time, enough excess catch had been spilled and crunched underfoot that shell replaced soil. That made the former dirt road, muddy in May and dull brown in December, transform into a pleasant glint of white and purple. Townspeople had fun teasing travelers who inquired about this peculiar, and quite beautiful, image. The tales differed based on the day and who was telling it. A favorite version involved an Ancient Celtic hunting expedition to the Horn of Africa that resulted in a massive acquisition of ivory. It was said that each man took at least two tusks from the slaughter. With this, they built the road.

On that road of ivory, in between the town and the bay, was a small shack with just enough room for a spatula, a frying pan and a man to put them to use. The aromas that emanated from inside carried medleys of sea and pasture from the anchorage outside the harbor to the town tavern.

Like any good entrepreneur, the shack owner knew the importance of location. The plot of land in question, for instance, had been selected for his business because it was perfectly situated to spread his fine cooking smells in all directions. To give thanks for such a spot, the shack owner made daily offerings to the winds, a ritual he carried out to show his appreciation for their willingness to spread the smell of his work. This 'ritual' took place in the morning hours with near military competency. The process was always the same. First, he would reheat a day-old batch of blood pudding gravy. Once it was warm, he would pour it into an old tin cup, the same old tin cup he used for each offering. Next, he would climb the highest hill overlooking the bay and toss the gravy over the cliffs in all four directions. For Auster, Boreus, Zephyr and Eurus...the four winds.

And what blood pudding it was.

There are a few times in our lives when the food we eat is an instant memory maker, when the sensation is so overwhelming, so delicious, that our taste buds go numb with an almost orgiastic delight and we remember where we were, who we were with, and what we were doing in that moment forever. It is that transcendent feeling that food so infrequently offers that takes one beyond the literal concept of eating. That sensation was experienced by every new patron who ordered blood pudding from that infamous shack just outside Drumcliffe.

"How long did you know him?" Cameron asked.

"Oh, I only went through Sligo twice, just passing by for the day or so. The second time I went was years later. And at that point, both the cook and his shack appeared to be gone. Naturally, I struck up a conversation with a local to corroborate this fact. The lady I asked informed me that I was partially correct and partially mistaken. She told me that the man who owned the shack moved his business inside town, away from the ivory road and far from the four winds. Upon further questioning, I came to learn that the reason for such a move was based on the sinking of the Princess Victoria. Apparently, he had loved ones on board when the ship sunk, and he came to blame the four winds for their betrayal in not keeping them safe. From that point forward, the pact was breached. The man wouldn't rely on the winds to spread his aromas any longer. When this conversation ended, I was determined to hear the true facts behind the story from the man himself, and get a good breakfast along the way. Unfortunately, my fellow travelers had other plans. The idea of venturing back into town just for breakfast was met with opposition. Looking back, I guess I can't really blame them. Every place we stopped to eat during our trip was advertised as "the best this" and "the best that" by someone in the car. The logical result of this would be skepticism for anything similarly advertised. Still, whether it was understandable or not, I needed to have that blood pudding. So, I told the driver to stop, and I got out of the car."

"And they just left you?" Cameron asked.

"Well, it wasn't like they just drove away. There was a brief conversation that got a bit heated. They said they had a train to catch. I said that trains would always come back, and if you thought about it, they were supposed to catch you, and that we may never come back here so it was worth staying a tad longer. Their inability to consider my reasoning made me see that these were not the type of people I wanted as friends any more. So, I slammed the door in their faces, and I never heard from them again. Well, that's not entirely true. One of them, a pretty girl with a yellow dress, had them stop the car some yards down the road. She joined me," the old man said. Then he went on to describe the woman with extraordinary detail. As he spoke, his face changed to the countenance of a person who looks at a cheerful photograph from years back and claims they are happy even though they are sad.

"What happened to the woman?" Cameron asked.

"She became my wife," the old man said.

"I find it hard to believe that we're designed to be with one person for the rest of our lives," Cameron said.

"That will change. When you get older, your loins concede to companionship," the old man said.

"That's what I hear, then I turn on the television and every other commercial is a man sitting in a bathtub watching the sunset as he eats a cereal bowl full of Viagra. So, I don't know. If I ever get a wife, I want her to be the subject of my fantasies, all of them, otherwise I won't marry her," Cameron said.

"Face those questions when you get there," the old man said. Then he asked Cameron if he was Catholic.

"Raised Catholic," Cameron said.

"You'll find Him again at some point or another, young man. I'm actually off to church as we speak, if you want to start the journey now."

"I'll pass," Cameron said.

"Then I suppose I should be going," the old man said.

"You're probably going to be late regardless," Cameron said.

"I go to Church every day at this time following my walk. The Father will understand when I explain why during confession," the old man said.

"Don't you think it's odd to take advice from a band of celibate men who voluntarily deprive themselves of living? I'm sure you have a wife, kids, grandchildren...whatever. I get the argument of bowing a knee to my elders, but I can't see the value of doing the same for them."

"My priest is from Congo. He's lived a life of unimaginable suffering. With only his wheel-barrel and his will, he saved many a friend's corpse from the buzzards in his home country. That's not living? This hero isn't worthy of giving advice? Don't be so childish to reduce a man's worth to their sexual proclivities. Any pubescent child can procreate," the old man said.

"Even so, the priesthood needs to go, or the rules need to be amended, especially when it comes to marriage. The alternative doesn't work. Saint Peter was married. There was no practice of celibacy before the fourth century, and these were the men who knew Christ, who were the true pillars of the Church. Oddly enough, the effect of such progressive reforms would be a return to the way things were. Strange concept in religious conversation," Cameron said.

The old man chose not to engage any further. Cameron took this to mean the conversation was over. As a result, he went back to the bottom of the tree where he had placed his socks and got ready to find a garbage can.

"This sight brings back memories," the old man said. He was looking back up at the shoes in the tree. Once again, Cameron stood corrected about the termination of any more conversation.

"Were you a cop on the gang unit?" Cameron asked.

Without answering, the old man went back into story-telling mode. He began to talk about a trip he took with his family many years ago. He defined the period in typical idyllic fashion the way most old people do when they speak of the past, as if despite world wars and genocide and a planet on the brink of nuclear annihilation for nearly half a century, they lived in a utopia, a utopia destroyed by incompetent progeny and even more incompetent progeny's progeny.

But back to the story. Back to the times, as the old man said, when vacations were less about cruises and cross-Atlantic flights and more about overstuffed station wagons zipping down the interstate. The latter was the method of travel for the old man and his then-young family. On this particular trip, they saw much of what America had to offer: the majestic overlooks of the Tetons; the empty fullness of the Grand Canyon; the rugged beauty of the Badlands; the resplendence of Mount Rushmore. Yet amidst all of these wonders, what the kids most appreciated along the way were the roadside critters, the areas ready for tag, the berry picking and the dandelions ready to be blown. Looking back, watching them enjoy those things, he couldn't help but wonder who was the parent, who was the teacher and who was the child.

There was no better instance of this on that trip than when they decided to turn back. It didn't happen according to any planned itinerary. Organization of that sort was never their strong suit. Everything was spur of the moment. That's why it was so fun.

This is how it happened. The old beat up station wagon was hauling ass across the Arizona desert at a steady 53 miles per hour. Out of that desert flatness eventually arose the Rockies, a mountain chain that made its kinfolk back East appear petty. Through the windshield the parents peered at them longingly, as this is what they came for. Then they looked at each other. Then they looked at the children behind them, still acting like angels but on the brink of turning into demons.

The old station wagon coughed. Its next dry, struggling gasp was the straw that broke the camel's back.

Having taken the northern route west, it was decided to hit

the prairies and see what they were all about on the way back east. Twelve or so hours into a drive dominated by infinite fields of grain and flatness, they took a gas exit and wound up in one of those quaint middle-America towns that screamed of a Sinclair Lewis novel. Somewhere within the aging cattle fences, where rusting howitzers dotted the landscape and meadows were parking lots for mud stained Fords, a gas station appeared.

With twilight fast approaching, it was critical to pull-in and refill the tank. The old man, then a young man, did his regular schmoozing with the locals at the pump. Always with an agenda, he was calculating whether the back roads he was taking would make him better time than the interstate.

On the other side of the road was a large field with fresh cut grass. It was mowed to about eight inches, just the right height for a passerby to realize a landscaper tended to the property but was inclined to keep it looking like a meadow. Grass heaps, the incense of any meadow maintained by man, were strewn across in every direction.

From the inside of the gas station window, the young man watched his young family dart across the fields. This included his three little ones and his wife, whom he said, with a smile, was the biggest kid of the lot. At first, they were playing some derivative tag game where the tops of the grass heaps provided a sort of safety zone from being 'it.' When tag ran its course, it was replaced by a footrace to the lone large tree in the middle of the meadow, now an emerging silhouette in the foreground of a darkening sky. Further and further they ran into the distance, until their bodies became blurs and blended into horizon line landscape.

"I walked over to them in the field with some snacks, figuring we'd have a late picnic lunch or an early dinner. I'll never forget that walk. A hidden mid-western Elysian Fields is what that place was. All of them there. All of them those ages forever, sitting Indian style around that tree playing duck-duck goose with no shoes on. When I go, that's where I hope I go," the old man said to Cameron.

"No shoes on?" Cameron asked.

"I found the absence of their footing strange myself. I don't know what it was, but I had an inkling to look above me for answers. What I saw was hauntingly beautiful. Hundreds, could have even been thousands, of shoes, hanging in the tree. 'Mommy did it first,' one of my little boys shouted in defense of his actions. She smiled and shrugged and begged me to do it, too."

"And did you?" Cameron asked.

"Nope," the old man said with despair. "I thought the whole thing ridiculous. Our finances were low. I was wearing my brown Clark loafers, the only thing I ever owned nice enough to show off. She grabbed my arm softly, I can still feel it today, and begged me to go along with it, saying something about experiences being more important than money. I walked back to the car in a huff and told them to follow."

"What was this tree?" Cameron asked.

"I wasn't sure at first. Then I did some research. It turns out these trees have some popularity on the other side of the country. There's a big one out in Reno. There's other well-known ones in Minnesota and Michigan, too," the old man said.

"What's the point of them?" Cameron asked.

The old man looked up at Cameron's pair of shoes dangling in the breeze just a tad out of reach. Then he said, "A shoe tree starts with a dreamer who hauls the first pair to the sky. Most of the time, that's where it ends. Sometimes, though, with the right set of circumstances, a couple passersby notice them and follow suit. That's when you have something, a type of domino effect that can last lifetimes. Pretty fascinating, especially if you get close enough to read some of the inscriptions people put on them. Before they throw them up, they write poems and dedications and wishes on them. Kind of a wishing well in the air if you will."

"Well, as great as that sounds, this one wasn't started with a dream, it was started with an accident," Cameron said.

"According to heathens like yourself, so too was the universe. That shouldn't make it any less marvelous," the old man said.

"It makes it more marvelous," Cameron said without pause.

The old man started walking away.

"Hey..." Cameron said. "Do you regret not throwing yours? Your shoes, I mean?"

The old man took a second to think about the question. Then he said, "After all these years, it's one of two real regrets."

"The other?" Cameron asked.

"Never going back to eat more blood pudding," the old man said.

3

Leaves

When the old man went on his way, Cameron continued down the road intent on finding a garbage can to dispose of his soiled socks. A loud irritating twang followed by the short putt-putt of a small motor caught his ear and directed his attention down the street in search of its cause.

The sound was easy to find.

A man wearing starched khakis was blowing one leaf across his emerald green lawn. Back and forth he went, blowing it ever so slowly, moving it a few feet and then going back to its previous resting place to correct the imperfections it left behind in the grass.

When the leaf got halfway across the lawn, the noise from the blower stopped. Puzzled, the man with starched khakis held the machine to his face for closer examination. When nothing seemed wrong, he revved it like he was starting the engine cold. He repeated the process a series of times until the blower responded.

After quickly bathing in the satisfaction of his tinkering, the man with starched khakis slung the tool onto his back and set out again to apprehend the lone leaf that beleaguered him. Bent on blowing rather than bending to pick it up, he elongated the process tenfold by chasing the uncooperative leaf back and forth across his lawn. His unhinged mouth and unblinking bulging eyes made him look more like an addict chasing a fix than a man doing yardwork.

"Here, I'll help you out, man," Cameron said after watching all that he could. Then he walked onto the lawn, picked up the leaf that pestered the man with starched khakis and handed it over. "I saw this was giving you some trouble."

The man with starched khakis paused for a moment before responding. He was looking at something behind Cameron. "Why'd you do that?" he said in a tone neither angry nor frustrated towards Cameron but very much confused. "I only needed to get it a few feet further to put it with the rest of them."

"What?" Cameron said.

The man with starched khakis pointed to the road behind Cameron. A lawn's worth of leaves was scattered in the street in front of the house next door.

"Why are they in front of your neighbor's house if they're your leaves?" Cameron asked.

"They aren't my leaves. They were on my property, but they weren't my leaves," the man with starched khakis said defensively, in a manner that suggested he had answered this question before. Then he directed Cameron towards the hedges that separated his lawn from his neighbors'. The man with starched khakis' side was perfectly landscaped. The other side was presentable but modest, becoming but certainly less micromanaged.

"So, you blow them from your property onto the street that

is in front of their house. Then you don't pick them up?" Cameron asked.

"It's not my problem," the man with starched khakis said. Again, Cameron felt he was looking behind him.

"If you were my neighbor, I think I'd call the town on you," Cameron said, even though he knew that was probably not true. In reality, he probably wouldn't do shit about it, just like the neighbors.

"Glad you aren't my neighbor then," the man with starched khakis said smiling. "But still...as I've told the town, not my leaves, not my problem."

"Couldn't you at least wait to begin this madness until later on in the day? It's early. Let everyone begin their morning in peace before you get to blowing like a madman. Even the landscapers give us that much. Where's your community etiquette?" Cameron said.

"Community etiquette. That house next to me destroyed community etiquette a long time ago," the man with starched khakis said. "I'm just following suit."

"And the rest of the neighbors. They don't have a say in being subjected to this racket?" Cameron asked.

"Collateral damage," the man with starched khakis said.

"This all seems pretty low," Cameron said.

"They should be happy I don't do more. What I should do is cut down those damn trees hanging over my property and be done with all it altogether," the man with starched khakis said. "Those damn hedges below them, too. Better yet, I should crush that goddamned statue," the man with starched khakis said.

The tiny limestone statue he referred to sat on the first porch step of the house next door. It was a strange looking figure, maybe a foot high, maybe a tad taller if its straw hat was taken into consideration. Key amongst its features was a massive open-mouthed grin. A cigar was stuck in between the two front teeth of that grin. At the feet of the statue was a decal of similar charm – a shot of whiskey.

"Does it have a name?" Cameron asked, immediately growing fond of the statue.

"Doesn't everything?" the man in starched khakis said.

"I think that's what this lawn needs," Cameron said.

"What this lawn needs is for you to stop stepping all over it," the man in starched khakis said in a friendly yet slightly agitated manner as he walked towards his driveway opposite the house with the statue. On his way there, he stopped various times to bend over and rearrange the grass blades Cameron had stepped on.

"You should ease up a little with the grass," Cameron said.

"Why's that?" the man with starched khakis said.

"It lacks personality. There's nothing appealing about a perfect lawn. Let a few weeds grow, man," Cameron said.

"Nothing like a man full of unsolicited suggestions," the man in starched khakis said.

"Sorry. I didn't mean to be rude. Someone with such a nice place who gets weekdays off doesn't need my advice," Cameron said.

"Is it a weekday? I didn't even know," the man with starched khakis said.

"Why's that?" Cameron said.

"I'm retired," the man with starched khakis said.

"You don't look old enough to be retired," Cameron said.

"Thank you," the man in starched khakis said, smiling.

"What did you do? Win the lotto?" Cameron asked.

"If I won the lotto, I wouldn't be living next to these bastards," the man in starched khakis said.

Cameron believed that the man with starched khakis' retirement resulted from economic success. Therefore, with hopes of obtaining some feedback to create some success of his own, he shared his current situation with the man with starched khakis. A former wide-eyed college graduate intent on pursuing the American dream, yet a year later, here he was, discontented and unskilled, unable to do much more than drag out the garbage and wonder whether his situation was his fault or society's or a little bit of both.

Cameron then asked the man with starched khakis whether he was happy in his business decisions and how they panned out.

"Do I look happy?" the man with starched khakis said as he wiped his brow. Cameron did not know how to answer. It was possible he could be both miserable and happy.

The man with starched khakis began to tell Cameron about his first day of retirement. "It's strange, you work all your life, and suddenly it just stops. Out of nowhere, it just stops. The thing is that people are meant to be doers. We need projects; we need...society. I've learned that the hard way in the year or so since I've been home."

"No wife?" Cameron asked.

"Divorced," the man in starched khakis said.

"No kids?" Cameron asked.

"College," the man with starched khakis said.

"Friends?" Cameron asked.

"Nope," said the man with starched khakis.

"Parents?" Cameron asked.

"My mom is gone. It's complicated with my dad," the man with starched khakis said.

"Siblings?" Cameron asked.

"A brother and a sister, I think. Sometimes I'm not so sure," the man with starched khakis said.

"As you continue to ponder that question, would you mind if I grab a drink from your hose? I'm a little dehydrated," Cameron said. The booze he enjoyed with the homeless-looking woman was turning his mouth to cotton.

"It's in the back yard. Just do me a favor, don't throw any Wiffle Balls back over the fence," the man with starched khakis said.

Cameron went in the backyard behind the white picket fence. When he did, he found the hose coiled against the side of the house right where the man with starched khakis said it would be. The cool water felt good on his lips despite the risk in putting his mouth to a hose that almost certainly applied pesticides to the lawn. That thought made him observe the grass, now beginning to stand in greater attention with the evaporation of more and more morning dew. His eyes were drawn to three tiny white orbs speckled across the otherwise emerald green backyard. Cameron walked a few feet closer to confirm that the orbs were Wiffle Balls.

This made Cameron smile. To him, there was no greater symbol of childhood, no greater repository of the fondest memories of his life, than playing ball in the backyard with his friends and family – just like these kids must have been doing. It was so simple then, so pleasurable, so easy.

Just then, a new ball landed in front of his feet. A minute or so later, another one dropped next to it.

"C'mon, asshole, that's two over in one at-bat," he heard a young boy's voice yell out.

"That's what happens when you pitch greatness on the inside corner," an even younger voice responded.

Cameron peered through the cracks in the stockade fence.

He saw the silhouettes of a group of boys playing in the back-yard. One of them was taking his time trotting around the bases. Halfway home and still at a snail's pace, Cameron saw the image of the pitcher gear up and hurl the ball in that direction.

He heard the hiss.

Then he heard the SMACK!

Then he heard the yelp.

The trotter fell to the ground. The rest of the players laughed. Then they quickly resumed their play. Meanwhile, the body of the boy continued to squirm between home and third.

Boys will be boys, Cameron thought.

Oh, how he missed those times, those days absent of long-ing, when youth was infinite and old age a fantasy. These thoughts made Cameron consider his chronology of aging. First, he saw a toddler rolling around in the dirt, smashing together rubber dinosaurs. In time, T-Rex was replaced by Legos, then Lincoln Logs and then balls and bats.

College graduation brought the most dramatic transition. Loneliness, unknown until then, became an everyday acquain-tance. He sighed at all he had taken for granted. Then he threw the Wiffle Balls back over the fence to the tune of shocked cries of appreciation. The act made Cameron feel good about himself. Better than he had in a while.

When he returned to the front lawn, he heard a glass bottle cap pop off a drink. His ears directed his eyes towards the noise. The man with starched khakis was on the first step of his stoop. His blower was in front of him, and a glass bottle was in his hand. The bottle contained an orange beverage called *South of Sunrise*. Then, with one massive and satisfying chug, it did not.

"I didn't take you for a Wiffle Ball player," Cameron said.

"Those kids never stop playing that fucking game. The balls

must've come over this morning. I got rid of the ones from last night," the man with starched khakis said.

"You didn't throw them back?" Cameron asked.

"No. We have an agreement. I pick them up and put them in a basket, and their mother comes and gets them once a day," the man with starched khakis said.

"Don't they just hop the fence?" Cameron asked.

"Mother lays down the law. They listen...sometimes," the man with starched khakis said.

"Then I guess I shouldn't have thrown them back?" Cameron said.

"What did I say?" the man with starched khakis said.

"I thought you were kidding," Cameron said.

The man with starched khakis launched the empty *South of Sunrise* bottle over the fence and into his neighbor's front yard. It was the same property where the kids were playing in the back. The ensuing crash told Cameron it slammed against a tree.

"Jesus, man. You don't get it. Nobody gets it. All I ever hear is them playing in that sandlot for a yard they have over there. It's non-stop. I can't take a piss in the middle of the night without worrying one of those damn balls is going to blast through my window," the man with starched khakis said.

"Did you take it up with their parents?" Cameron asked.

"I told their father that if I wanted to live next to a playground then I would've moved next to one," the man with starched khakis said.

"And what did he say?" asked Cameron.

"He isn't exactly receptive to my complaints nowadays. So, I deal with his wife," said the man with starched khakis, "which has created its own slew of problems."

"Like what?" Cameron asked.

"Use your imagination," the man with starched khakis said.

"Sounds like quite the predicament," Cameron said.

"You don't know the half of it," said the man with starched khakis. "Good talking to you, buddy."

Then he slapped Cameron on the shoulder and went inside.

4

La Guillotine

Since the street was covered by a canopy of trees, Cameron did not have to worry about burning the soles of his feet. Morning still had life left in it, so even in places where sunlight crept through the leafy barrier, it did so with limited intrusion. That made the short trek to the tiny beach parking lot, which Cameron had resolved to reach despite the morning's setbacks, simple enough to manage. If nothing else, there he would certainly find a garbage can for his socks.

A small tractor-trailer was parked on the far side of the tiny beach parking lot when he arrived. The yellow machine next to it, called a Bobcat, which was virtually a mini bulldozer-tractor, answered any questions regarding what it had hauled. Meanwhile, a two-man crew was busy at work in the parking lot. They were repairing a floatation dock that was probably part of the wreckage from the last storm.

Cameron recalled a conversation he had with a dark-skinned Caribbean man wearing a Columbian vueltiao the day before that storm. While the rest of the block was preparing for the Second Coming, the Caribbean man with the vueltiao was mowing his Eden of a lawn with a reel mower in the late afternoon sun, pausing periodically at the end of each finished row to tend to his flowers. Inside this outpost of paradise, large leafy plants bordered by Casablanca lilies draped themselves over various sun-baked trellises. A tiny central gate guarded by sunflowers and an overhanging honeysuckled arbor served as the entryway to the modest bungalow behind it.

Cameron had been in the area hauling sandbags into a basement cellar to prevent water damage from the same approaching storm. The house with that basement cellar was located across the street from the bungalow where the Caribbean man with the vueltiao lived. When he started to take the sandbags off the truck and into the house, the Caribbean man with the vueltiao started pointing and laughing at him.

"Quite the mower you got there," Cameron said, retaliating in the only way he knew how.

"Next year, I'm upgrading to a goat," said the Caribbean man with the vueltiao.

"By the looks of this storm, there won't be a next year," Cameron said.

"Armageddon will come someday, my friend, but weathermen won't be able to forecast it in advance," said the Caribbean man with the vueltiao.

"So, you're just going to go about your day as if there's no storm coming?" Cameron asked.

"It's coming whether I go inside and watch the clock or I continue working. Filling a few sandbags won't change that," said the Caribbean man with the vueltiao.

"Not much of a worrier?" Cameron asked.

"I'm used to this sort of thing. When storms like what's coming dropped down in my home country, they weren't even newsworthy. We learn that they come and go, and if you learn to respect them, they generally leave you alone. When they don't, and it takes the house, you just build it back up. That's why I have such a simple structure. I maintained that philosophy during its construction."

So, the storm came. And what the Caribbean man with the vueltiao said proved true. Compared to what was expected, minimum damage ensued. A few old trees fell onto even older telephone wire transformers; a moderate storm surge forced some houses to be elevated onto stilts; and lastly, the canal flooded, thereby ruining the integrity of an already dilapidated boardwalk dock. Contractors across the area vied for the opportunity to reconstruct the dock. Few, however, had the patience to navigate the labyrinth of bureaucratic red tape that awaited them once the job was theirs. Therefore, the contract was repeatedly subcontracted until it finally fell into the hands of the only qualified person willing to put shovel to soil. When those in the industry learned who it was, they all responded in a similar fashion. They laughed and said he does the best work, but he's painfully slow and completely crazy.

A tall young blond man and a Latino about a decade his senior were on the job site when Cameron got there. Together, they loaded debris from the damaged dock into a wheelbarrow and hauled it over to the dumpster.

Each time another successful batch was unloaded, they switched places so each had a turn with the wheelbarrow. Due to their competitive nature, they also increased the size of the next haul each time they finished one. A productive plan at first, it was ineffective within a few shifts. As is common on construction sites, testosterone won over their wits. The tall blond young man took a load that was too heavy to handle and fell on his way to the dumpster. This caused him to wince in pain, roll over and sit on the street with his back up against the side of the dumpster. "Fuck this shit, man. Fuck!" he said as he wiped the blood from the scrapes on the side of his stomach and hands. Then he took out a pack of Newports from his pocket. When he realized there were no smokes left in the box, he made a fist and punched the ground. He shook his head and grimaced at the blood now running from his knuckles as a result.

"That's just what I need right now. Just what I need."

The Latino man reached into his pocket and handed the tall young blond man a new box of Newports.

"I didn't know you smoked, man, thanks," said the tall young blond man.

"I don't. Damage control," the Latino man said.

"You're the best. He really is," the tall young blond man said to assure Cameron of the truth of his statement.

"I know this job has you, what is it, buggin'?" the Latino man said.

"You know it. We fucking work all day, and we get shit. Whoever heard of eighty dollars a day for thirteen hours of work? That's some bullshit," the tall young blond man said as he ran his hands through his hair. A summer of outdoor work had bronzed the skin that covered up his bulging muscles. It also gave him a cornfield of blond hair that fell freely over his ears. Cameron contrasted it to his own hairdo or lack thereof, which was brown and receded in tire track fashion down his scalp. Meanwhile the Latino man shook his head in agreement with what the tall young blond man was complaining about. Bellyaching about work hours and poor pay were common channels of communication on work sites for those who otherwise had nothing in common.

More blood from the tall young blond man dripped down

his thigh and saturated his long tube socks just below the knee. "These were new socks, too. I'd like to see him pay for them with that workman's comp and shit he always brags about giving us," the tall young blond man said.

Tired of the Latino just yessing him to death, the tall young blond man looked up at Cameron watching them and engaged him in conversation.

"This boss of ours thinks he's god's gift to earth because he pays us on the books, doesn't hire illegals and provides workman's comp," the tall young blond man said.

"Sounds good to me" Cameron said. "Maybe I should work for him."

"It sounded pretty good to me at first, too," the tall young blond man said as he flicked the ash off the end of his cigarette. But don't be fooled..." he pointed to Cameron, his face cockeyed because he was facing the sun and his throat was full of smoke. "Our boss...he's a scumbag. He works us to the bone and gives us eighty dollars a day. Mexicans won't even work for that shit. Other than this idiot here," the tall young blond man continued. When he did, Cameron began to realize that this young man, despite his age, his height and his muscular structure, was just a boy.

"Speak of the devil," the tall young blond man said as a red pickup pulled up in front of them and two men got out. A tall, pot-bellied, slightly overweight and loosely muscled man with a bad comb-over hardly covering his bald spot was driving. The man in the passenger seat was generic looking. "I bought you guys drinks and snacks," he said. It was clear from how he carried himself that he was in charge, that he was the Contractor.

"I thought you went to do fi chi?" the tall young blond man

said as he quickly grabbed a coffee and coffee cake from the brown deli bag and sat against the wheel of the pickup.

"I did do my fi chi," the contractor said, being openly disparaging of the tall young blond man's idiocy whether the latter knew it or not. "Dewayne grabbed me on my way back from the beach when he was coming back with the stuff."

"Figures. That bum Dewayne will do anything to escape doing work," the tall young blond man said. "Hey Dewayne, while he's getting the stuff out of the truck, why don't you come over and help us out," the tall young blond man said.

Dewayne looked at him with the face of an officer being disrespected by an underling.

"What did I tell you about talking to me in the morning before I had my hot chocolate and had time to meditate? I don't know much, but if there's one thing in this world I do know, it's a slacker when I see one. Focus on your own work," Dewayne said.

"You tell em DeeeeWayne," the contractor said in a tone that was equally disparaging as the one he just used to address the tall young blond man. He made these comments as he searched for a lost pencil in the front seat of the truck. Nobody bothered to tell him there was one in his mouth.

"I don't give a shit what Dewayne tells me," the tall young blond man said.

Dewayne took a deep breath, closed his eyes and put his hands to the sky. "Oh, grant me the patience to deal with this boy. Loooooooooord have mercy." His raspy church-yelling was as much an orchestra of the body as a sample of his vocal register.

"If I've said this once, I've said this a thousand times. Do your job, boy, and I'll do mine," Dewayne said.

"And what exactly is your job? I've been trying to figure that out ever since you started working here," the tall young blond man said.

"I'm a utility guy. I do what's needed at the time. Right now, I'm babysitting," Dewayne said.

"Bullshit. No parents would let you anywhere near their kids," the tall young blond man said.

"Kid's got a point, Dewayne," the contractor said.

"Say what you want, I know a bad kid when I see one. I used to be a bad kid, that's how I know that's how I know that's how I know. That boy needs an attitude adjustment. And he better figure out that adjustment sooner than later, or we should fire his ass. LOOORD HAVE MERCY!" Dewayne said to the contractor loud enough for everyone to hear.

"How about you? Looking for a job?" the contractor asked Cameron.

"Why do you think I need a job?" Cameron asked.

"I've been around long enough to know you fit the profile," the contractor said.

"I think I'll pass," Cameron said.

"Why? Doesn't square with life plans?" the contractor asked.

"I'd have to know what those plans are to be able to answer that question," Cameron said.

"Besides those who have a real gift, like a Michael Phelps, it can take time, a lot of trial and error. For me, it took years of office work before I realized that I hated it and wanted to work outside with my hands. My coworkers knew it before me. But what they see doesn't matter. You need to see it for yourself," the contractor said.

"Do you regret not changing careers earlier?" Cameron asked.

"In the summer. Not in the winter," the Contractor said. "Now, who's mixing that cement?"

"I thought Jose was doing that," Dewayne said.

"I am. And my name isn't Jose. I haven't started because you said you wanted to show me a better way to do it because if there's one thing in this world you know, it's concrete," the Latino man said.

"Well, whoever made the concrete over here, it's terrible," the contractor said as he examined some in his hand from the pile. When the examination ran its course, he plopped the cement blob on the ground and watched it splatter. Then the contractor lowered down onto his stomach, face to the concrete, and watched the way the material rushed to and from the splat. He ordered them all to do the same – even Cameron – who he assured would benefit from his lecture on cement whenever he worked with it someday.

The contractor went on to explain how the art of cement-making should not be taken for granted. He noted that the very process that creates the cement for a dock boardwalk here had also been used to create the Hoover Dam and the Roman Pantheon. For all spawn from the same humble beginnings – from the primordial goop inside of a wheelbarrow – and can only be harnessed by the combination of man and spade and a few buckets of water.

"Three things: one, two, three, come together to make cement. Lime, like the rock not the fruit, Jose, rubble, and volcanic ash, which is also called Pozzolon by the Italians. Named, as I'm sure none of you know..."

"Because it was near Mount Mesuvious," said the tall blond young man.

"YES!" the contractor said ecstatically. "Well, almost. You see, Pozzolon was the small village nestled in the foothills of Mount Vesuvius where they first recorded finding this ash. You see, when you work with cement, you're working with history, contributing to humanity's future. Do not discount what you are doing as some ruffian task. Think about it. Everything modern man has, from aqueducts to fortresses to the very ground we stand on and plan to rebuild, it's all cement. That brings me back to this crap in front of me. The Greeks built the Colossus with this shit. Show it some respect. Remember what we're building here."

"A sidewalk," the tall young blond man said.

"Not just a sidewalk, not just a piece of a dock," the contractor said. "But a tribute to man's partnership with the sea. Remember, architecture is not just sketching blueprints of buildings. It's also what we're doing right here. We're all architects! Don't let anyone tell you otherwise!"

"I've repeated that to this boy here all along, but he wouldn't listen. I'll make sure they don't screw it up again," Dewayne said.

"You do that, Dewayne," the contractor said.

"Wouldn't it be easier if we could use a mixer instead of shovels and a wheelbarrow?" Dewayne asked.

"Low on funds, boys. And the Bobcat gets fixed before the mixer. You know that," the contractor said. "For now, we'll have to stick to the old stuff. Before we get started with that, though, someone help me get those beams out of the truck."

He first looked at Dewayne.

"Gotta finish my hot chocolate or you know how I get," Dewayne said.

Then he looked at the Latino man.

"Still working on my coffee," he said.

Then he looked at the tall blond young man.

"Seniority, bud. Get those beams down," the contractor said.

"I'll help him out," Cameron said.

"Sorry. I can't have you get hurt on the job. I'll do it until he gets enough," the contractor said. "Then the other two can take care of what's left."

"Until I get enough?" the tall young blond man repeated to Cameron. "Sure."

Together, the contractor and the tall young blond started moving the beams. The tall young blond man smoked a cigarette as they worked.

"Why do me and my workers all have to inhale carcinogens because of you? If you need a smoke break, just ask," the contractor said. Then he went on to interrogate the tall young blond man, asking why he smoked, if he cared that doing so was inconsiderate, if his parents smoked, how people with a limited income could waste money on poisoning themselves and so on. The tall young blond man argued that smoking kept him calm and at this point in his life, that mattered most. From afar, Cameron wondered what the tall young blond man was like angry if his current state passed for calm.

Inserted in between the contractor's complaints about the tall young blond man's habits were his comments that, despite age, he was still a better lifter. The contractor was clear to attribute this to his technique. He said that because he lifted with an Olympic deadlifting stance, he could carry more weight, and therefore more beams, without tiring. On the contrary, the tall young blond man lifted with his lower back and was injury prone and unstable.

"Brain over brawn," the contractor said.

Still, they went steady for a while. Then the contractor slowly began to edge towards the middle of the beams when lifting. This allowed his exhausted forearm to rest as more weight transferred to the tall young blond man. Unfortunately for the contractor, the tall young blond man was a hulk, so slight alterations in weight distribution were inconsequential.

"I'm not going to ask you again, can you get that cigarette out of my face? Just break right now," the contractor said. "I can't take the smoke anymore."

"There's no reason to stop now. Only a little bit left," the tall young blond man said.

"My lungs think differently. Now go, other side of the street until you're done," said the contractor.

"You guys take over for us since he needs a break," the contractor said to the Latino and Dewayne. Then the contractor went over to the brown deli bag on the truck to finish his coffee. The tall young blond man, now settled twenty or so yards from the rest of the crew, raised his middle finger to the contractor as soon as his back was turned.

"What did I tell you about Styrofoam cups, Dewayne?" the contractor said.

"PLASTOCENE!" the tall young blond man yelled proudly from his exile across the street.

"That's right!" the contractor said. "They're made with Plastocene, a plastic created from petroleum. If I wanted to have a glass of gasoline, I'd have gone to Exxon Mobile and put my mouth on the nozzle. I can't drink this." Then he emptied his coffee onto the ground.

"I don't understand," Dewayne said.

"That's because you're a fucking idiot," the tall blond young man said. "Plastocene is a carcinogenic. That shit will give you cancer," the tall blond young man said, crossing back over to join the rest of the crew. Evidently, he had finished his cigarette.

"Worse than that, by purchasing these products, we're helping the damn corporations that are killing this country," the ontractor said.

"I don't understand," Cameron said.

"Don't get him started, son. Lord have Mercy if he gets going on that topic," Dewayne said.

"I like to consider myself a bit of a Renaissance man," the contractor began. He spoke to Cameron as he grabbed his hand hoe and went to work digging a little trench and picking out loose material that would disrupt the smoothness of the surface area. The rest went back to work doing their respective tasks, only listening enough to respond if needed. "And as a Renaissance man, I see things before they happen. Mainly, I do this by analyzing historical trends and comparing them to the present day. Though many historical analogies can be made to today, it is the French Revolution that appears most significant in my eyes. The French experienced a brutal economic hardship leading up to 1789. There was no food, infrastructure development stalled, debts rose, national exports declined. To make matters worse, France's best client was its worst enemy – Great Britain. This was especially true with textiles, which were far cheaper to make in Britain than in France. In addition to that, the tax system was corrupt. King Louis XVI, no matter his enforcement measures, failed to get the clergy and the nobility to pay up. The rich resented this and found other ways to avoid contributing their fair share. All of this combined to leave the labor force angry and unemployed and with the burden of paying taxes for the entire country."

"Sounds like a struggle every time period has faced in every country everywhere," Cameron said.

"Perhaps, but the lesson remains. The FUCKING CORPORATE BEHEMETHS have been ripping off the country for too long. Now it's reaching a tipping point like it did in France. And the truth is, none of this really affects me. I'm secure. I have money. But I really feel for young people now. Look around, opportunity is gone, opportunity for a child to be more successful than their parents, gone. Imagine that, here in the United States. Our City on a Hill. Fucking CORPORATE BEHEMOTHS! They took it from us." As he said this, the contractor went on slamming his pick into the ground with increasing intensity, almost to the point of tears.

"I don't think the situation is as dreary as that," Cameron said. "Lack of opportunity presents opportunity. Who knows, maybe when young people notice jobs are scarce, they'll go back to the drawing board and pursue their passions. It could be for the benefit of all of us. Your predictions of disaster could be strewn with a dash of promise."

"You don't get it, kid. It doesn't matter what you do. Even if you split the atom, the CORPORATE BEHEMOTHS will take it from you. They control everything – from our food, to our clothes, to the fuel we put in our cars. Did you know that there was a model electric car out in 1834? Thomas Davenport of Vermont invented it. Did you also know that in 1917 we had a hybrid car already built? But leave it to the CORPORATE BEHEMOTHS, the damn CORPORATE BEHEMOTHS to stall such progression. They dirtied our planet, had us kill each other, and traded our money away. The thing is, when things are okay, they can get away with it, they can sweep their shit under the rug. But I think the gig's almost up. And when it is, I'll be the first one shouting BRING BACK LA GUILLOTINE!!!

"Before you start the revolution, remember this, the radicals in the French Revolution met the same fate as those they executed. Danton was killed. After him, Robespierre," Cameron stated.

"Robespierre does not deserve to be placed in the same category as those he beheaded," the contractor said.

"Why's that?" Cameron asked.

"He was a product of his environment," the contractor said.

"Isn't everyone a product of their environment?" Cameron asked.

"Hear me out," the contractor said. "Before French Fascists got hold of the country, Robespierre was a successful lawyer, an outspoken voice for the emancipation of Jews and slaves and against...the DEATH PENALTY! HAHA! How men change. But he did what he had to do, like WE have to do!" he said passionately, waving his hand hoe in the air like a rebellious peasant. "The mob was only an engine. The ends justified the means!"

"And the same thing would happen now as it did in France. The executions would occur more frequently on the basis of less and less facts. Regular people, rather than your CORPORATE BEHEMOTHS, would suffer," Cameron said. "If there is any common thread of history, it is that the common person suffers most in any great struggle."

"My Bobcat and my mixer are broken. Now my crew will have to do the demolition by hand. I suppose the commoner is the victim behind this struggle as well," the contractor said.

"The Bobcat, how long till it's fixed?" Cameron asked.

"A few weeks probably," the contractor said.

"Will you be finished here by then?" Cameron asked.

"I'm not the best estimator when it comes to those sorts of things," the contractor said.

"I see that when it comes to the future, you're better at predicting social revolution than the pace of construction?" Cameron said.

"I suppose one is easier to guess than the other," the contractor said.

"I'll believe it when I see it," Cameron said.

And then he was off.

5

The Blurred Memories of a
Straight-edge Junkie

Cameron walked over to the restrooms closer to the beach. It was a little later in the morning, so he figured they would now be open. This assumption proved correct. Cameron pushed past the rickety old plywood door and stood within the dark rusty frame of the bathroom stall that was a little shorter than the top of his head. Then he squared himself to the bowl.

When he exited the stall, he turned to the vanity and the dirty mirror above it. Cobwebs draped across both top corners. A tiny hopper window above the stall and the crack under the door provided just enough light to see himself clearly. It was amazing how long he'd lived without having a conscious understanding of his appearance. He wondered why that was. It probably had something to do with his thinking that valuing his appearance was shallow. Of course, this supposed wisdom did not transfer to his thinking about other people, who he inevitably judged by the way they looked. Talk about a double standard. It also probably had something to do with his occasional fear, a fear that could turn into obsession, of being gay.

An ultra-concern about the way he looked, to him, would have given that fear more legs to stand on.

To be clear, he wasn't gay. He was just scared, scared to face his obsessive scary thoughts, scared to see what these thoughts revealed about himself; scared that his faith in himself, in who he was, could be so compromised that even something as clear to him as his sexuality could be put in doubt. That was frustrating, if not devastating, if not terrifying. It made him look at the mirror and wonder what certainty would next become uncertain. Would he start to debate the color of his skin, whether he breathed air, whether the sky was above and the land was below? Ultimately, when you can't trust yourself, it makes it impossible to trust anyone else. Relationships end or never begin.

To escape these particular tortures and obsessions, as well as many others, Cameron dappled in his fair share of psychiatric medications over the years. On and off the drugs he went. Each doctor had their own opinion on what it was and how to "fix" it. Each drug they prescribed created its own sort of mental state and, to an extent, performed the job intended. They limited the obsessions, stabilized his moods and manias and reduced some of the panic. These positive effects, however, were not without downsides. They extinguished libido. They made serviceable erections nearly impossible. Sex became a pressure-packed ordeal. Performance-related excuses accompanied every physical affair.

Zombification was another side effect of the psychiatric medications. There were days, some months, even years of his life that felt draped in a curtain of the surreal. People would fade out of focus when he spoke to them like his eyes were two broken camera lenses. It took him a long time to learn how to articulate these sensations to therapists. Eventually, he came to describe it as going through life with a body that functioned like it was always the most humid of days, where merely walking though air felt like trouncing though sludge.

All in all, he considered his past the blurred memories of a straight-edge junkie. He kept that phrase close to him because it kept him cognizant of the fine lines between someone who was a respectable "patient" trying to help themselves, and someone who was an addict screaming for mercy one second in the public square and then telling the world to fuck itself a minute later. The latter used drug dealers, the pharmacies of the street, to dull their pain, to get through the day. Cameron had the currency to get his support from a licensed professional with a swirly signature. To him, at the end of the day, the difference appeared to be nothing more than perspective. And perspective was not a good enough reason for the drastic difference in how society viewed one versus the other.

These thoughts ushered in familiar anxieties, about work, about getting a job, about keeping that job, and about liking it. He hated being so afraid. If others were given his situation they would be excited about the future. That made him feel like he had done something wrong. Suddenly, he felt guilty.

These thoughts accompanied his walk back up the Old Shaoling Road where he saw a little boy with a heart shaped head sitting on a curb tossing a baseball to himself. Such a sight raised Cameron's spirits. So, too, did the fact that the street was damp where he played catch. If not, the asphalt would have been intolerable on his bare feet, and he would have kept to the grass like Cameron coming towards him, who also had no shoes on. A brief lapse in concentration, probably from looking at Cameron approaching, was all it took for the little boy with the heart-shaped head's toss to escape his glove, causing the ball to roll across the street. Since it was closer to Cameron than the boy with the heart-shaped head, Cameron went and retrieved it.

The street was hotter than expected when he did so, and his feet paid the price. His dignity did as well, as any effort he mustered to act tough in front of the youth was eventually stymied when the burning sensation overtook him. Right after he picked up the ball, he winced at the pain and darted for the other side of the street on his tippy toes. Cameron's sigh of relief after completing the task made the boy with the heart-shaped head chuckle. This caught Cameron by surprise, for he thought the little boy with the heart-shaped head was too young to chuckle.

"Can't find anyone else to play?" Cameron asked playfully to the boy with the heart-shaped head as he signaled for him to toss the ball over.

The boy with the heart-shaped head's eyes lit up. He threw the ball over to him. Cameron wondered if what he was doing crossed the barriers of what was socially permissible. Sad as the world had become, a stranger would perceive the sight of him playing catch with a little boy that he did not know as highly suspicious.

"My brother and his friends took off to the deli to get food, so nobody's around," the boy with the heart-shaped head said.

"Why didn't you go?" Cameron asked.

"I went in the house to grab some money. They said they'd wait for me in the driveway over there. When I came back, all their bikes were gone. They must've forgotten I was inside and took off before realizing I wasn't there," the boy with the heart-shaped head said.

"Why didn't you hop on your bike and try and catch up?" Cameron asked.

"I'm not allowed to go that far on my own," the boy with the heart-shaped head said. "I just hope my brother remembers to get me something while he's there."

"How long have you been waiting for them?" Cameron asked.

"Well, we were playing Wiffle Ball in the back, and I'd just knocked some balls over the fence into our neighbors' yard. My brother and his friends were pissed. They don't like to talk to that neighbor. Neither does my dad. So, I guess I can't blame them for going on ahead without me. I mean, I did spoil the game," the little boy with the heart-shaped heart said.

"Well, let's start a new game. Toss it here," Cameron said.

As with any catch between people unfamiliar with each other, there is an experimental few throws where each monitors the other's ability. At first, balls are tossed back and forth, nice and slow. This went on for a little. But once Cameron saw the boy with the heart-shaped head could play, he started throwing harder and harder until they were zooming the ball back and forth from both ends of the property. Cameron tested his skills with pop ups and grounders, subconsciously trying to evaluate if he was better at that age than the boy in front of him. With each successful grounder that he gobbled up, the little boy with the heart-shaped head taunted Cameron. When Cameron heard this, he thought how all he needed to do was throw it too hard and break the kid's nose in response to the taunting. That would be fun to recount in police custody. 'Do you know that child?' 'No Sir.' 'Why were you playing with a little boy you didn't know?' 'It seemed fun.' 'Why don't you come with us.'

For someone his age, the boy with the heart-shaped head was exceptional. This combined with the fact that he had quite the little ego explained why he was pegged in the face. Since the showboating bothered him, even made him a little jealous despite not wanting to admit it, Cameron could only imagine how it affected an older kid dealing out homeruns – homeruns that resulted in lost balls and fewer games. No wonder they ditched him.

The more difficult Cameron made the throws, the easier it seemed the boy with the heart-shaped head fielded them and threw them back. From the throws back, Cameron's hand was beginning to suffer. Even so, he kept quiet. He'd rather break bones than give the little boy with the heart-shaped head the satisfaction of knowing he threw too hard for him to catch without a glove. Maybe it was Cameron's grimaces that gave it away, but the little boy with the heart-shaped head smiled and accepted what he saw as a tacit challenge to lay down his leather as well.

So, by means of a bare-fisted baseball catch, Cameron faced off against a nine-year old over the question of manhood. Back and forth they tossed, each throw increasing in distance and speed. To his surprise, neither participant acknowledged their pain. On a similar note, Cameron also ignored the alarms inside his head that urged him to act maturely. Hell with it. He wasn't going to let some wise ass little shit beat him in a game of catch.

On the next throw back to him, Cameron caught the ball in stride, crow-hopped and blazed as hard a ground ball as he could muster across the lawn. Midway to its target, the ball skipped up, it must have hit a rock or something, and lazily popped into the air for an easy grab.

"More like that," the little boy with the heart-shaped head said with knowledge that the throw included some additional mustard. In response, Cameron repeated his crow-hop and launched a ball as high as he could into the clouds. Its path of descent brought it into the overhanging trees on the other side of the property. Once it bounced off the first branch of one of the trees, the little boy with the heart-shaped head abandoned pursuit. Meanwhile, the ball pin-balled down towards the grass where it eventually landed just to the right of the little limestone ghoulish statue. Any closer and the statue's top hat would've doubled as a landing pad and cracked to pieces.

"Why didn't you try and catch it?" Cameron asked.

The little boy with the heart-shaped head grabbed his right foot and hopped on the other. Cameron noticed a slit in his big toe. "How did that happen?" Cameron asked.

"There's a broken glass bottle over by the tree," said the little boy with the heart-shaped head.

Cameron looked over at the tree. His glance revealed a half-broken bottle of *South of Sunrise*. "You okay?" he asked.

"I'm okay. But my dad is going to flip. He knows our neighbor chucks his garbage over the fence. Still, it's better my foot got hit than the statue. The ball missed it by a few inches when it fell from the branches. My dad loves that thing more than anything, especially lately."

"Why?" Cameron asked as he looked at the limestone ghoul statue.

"Not sure exactly. He's had it forever. All I know is that he comes home every night and sits and talks to it while he drinks. He says it watches out for us. That it watches out for him. Sometimes late at night, I can hear him crying out there with it. The more I think about it, the more I wish someone just broke it," the little boy with the heart-shaped head said.

"Weird," Cameron said.

"It's even weirder how much he changes when he comes back inside after being around it," said the boy with the heart-shaped head.

Suddenly, an ice cream truck made a sharp turn onto the street burning rubber and blaring Iron Maiden.

A pack of five boys on bikes peddled behind the truck as fast as they could. 'STOP, FAT MAN! STOPPP!'

The enormous man sitting in the ice cream truck zoomed past Cameron and the little boy with the heart-shaped head wearing a wide, wicked grin. As he did so, he swerved back and forth down the street. Apparently, he was making a game out of coaxing the boys to chase him. This observation was confirmed when, on two different occasions, he let the kids catch up to him only to drive away right after they got off their bikes to place an order.

When the kids saw Cameron and the boy with the heart-shaped head, they suspended their chase and pulled up next to them on their bikes. They skidded hard, leaving burnt tire tracks in the asphalt. Two of the five didn't have bikes. They sat on the handlebars of one bike and the pegs of another and jumped off before their respective riders slammed the brakes. Seeing this, the ice cream truck up ahead ended the game and parked in a manner that assumed some permanency down in the tiny beach parking lot opposite where the construction workers continued their labors. A yellow overhang unrolled out where the front window was. Lines started forming. The music switched from Iron Maiden to a merrier, more customary jingle.

"Why didn't you stop him?" one of the boys said. It was the same kid who yelled down the street to the fat ice cream man. After he said this, he punched the little boy with the heart-shaped head in the arm with an intensity that was hard enough to be painful but light enough to also be playful. "He took our money after we ordered and drove away without giving us our stuff."

"Didn't you already eat at the deli?" the boy little boy with the heart-shaped head asked.

"Nah, we saw him coming down the block so we tried to get something from him instead," the boy who punched him said.

"Yeah, this guy needed his damn *South of Sunrise,* and you can't get it anywhere but from him," a boy said who was clearly the little boy with the heart-shaped head's brother.

The whole lot of them had sharp tongues, a trait Cameron appreciated. No doubt products of their environment, these were the neighborhood kids that hadn't gone to camp. Why they didn't was evident in their presentation. They fit into three categories. The first were those with the raggedy clothes who rode on handlebars and pegs. They couldn't afford going. The second were those who were clean and kempt, who looked like they had mothers at home who cared but believed the streets were a nursery needed to raise a child. The third and strangest case was that of the boy who punched the boy with the heart-shaped head. He had the nicest bike and the nicest clothes. Underneath these material items, though, was a physical body that signaled neglect and a mouth that lacked the oversight of a proper guardian. Altogether, these traits made this boy a scamp, if there ever was one.

"Who the fuck is this?" the Scamp asked, casually referring to Cameron.

"Shut-up, dude," the older brother of the boy with the heart-shaped head said. "He can't help it," he said to Cameron. "His mouth's a second anus. In time, you get used to the diarrhea that spills out of it."

"No problem," Cameron said. "Hey, how did this guy manage an Italian ice? I didn't see the ice cream man stop."

"That's because he didn't. We picked him up on the way back because we saw him outside his house. That's from his freezer. The fat man doesn't sell Italian ices. Everyone knows that. He says it's an insult to Italy that something with its name on it tastes so bad. God forbid he sells something to disgrace the Italians. Fat fucker stops me from getting my sugar by not stopping," the Scamp said. "We should retaliate."

"I have some leftover water balloons," the little boy with the heart-shaped head mumbled.

"Good. We'll crush him!" the Scamp said. "He'll never drive by us without stopping again."

The boys spent the next ten minutes prospecting potential faucets in the area. While they did this, the boy with the heart-shaped head ran back into his house to grab the balloons. Along with the ammo, he returned with more appropriate footwear for the upcoming expedition: a Band-Aid for his cut foot, some socks and a pair of black *Nikes* with orange stripes. As he put them on, the rest of the boys divvied up the balloons and dashed back to different backyard hoses of neighbors not home. Only the Scamp ventured towards the man in starched khakis' house next door.

"Why the hell are you going over there?" the older brother of the little boy with the heart-shaped head said, calling to him as he walked away.

"Why not?" the Scamp replied.

"Don't be an idiot. You remember the last time you went over there," the older brother of the little boy with the heart-shaped head said.

Seeing Cameron was confused by this comment, the little boy with the heart-shaped head informed him of what happened last time. The neighbor blew his top, screaming and yelling and threatening to call the cops the next time any one of them came into his yard. If they wanted balls, they could send their mother over.

"That's just because he wants to slam your mom, dude. It gives him an excuse to have her over," the Scamp said.

"Believe me. I've seen them together when nobody else is around."

"Or it's because he saw you jerking off in the hedges when you were supposed to be taking care of our flowers when we were on vacation," the older brother of the little boy with the heart-shaped head said, laughing.

"He never saw me, dude!" the Scamp said.

"He told my mom about you, man," the older brother of the little boy with the heart-shaped head said. "C'mon, leave his house alone. We need help in the back to fill up these balloons."

The Scamp reluctantly complied and followed them into their backyard. Cameron wished them the best of luck in the upcoming altercation but declined their invitation to follow. To the tune of being called a "pussy" by the Scamp, he walked back down the street towards the ice cream truck. He figured that he may have been too old to participate in the balloon bombardment, but he was not too old to watch. To better his upcoming spectator experience, he began to think about how he could barter for refreshments since he had no money. For, a frozen treat with some *South of Sunrise* to wash it down sounded pretty good right about now.

6

South of Sunrise

Appropriately, the fat ice cream man named his business "Fat Man Ice Cream." The logo on his truck portrayed that description. Each side was adorned with a massive caricature of his face. The work of art was not only proportional, it served its purpose. For whatever reason, it made people want a Popsicle.

The line for ice cream formed from thin air in the beach parking lot. Some customers came from behind backyard fences. Others paused their gaming consoles and emerged from nearby basements. Cameron looked at the sad lot of them and had one of his cynical senior moments that should have been reserved for someone three times his age. How wasteful. These kids had the skill to wield the power of modern technology and chose to utilize it for *Halo* and *Call of Duty*. Where were their real-world passions? Their sports, their instruments, their paintbrushes? "Fool's gold," he remembered hearing someone say about smart phones. Only humanity could take a perfect device to enhance human intelligence and use it to make people stupid.

It is worthy of mention that the two people at the front of the ice cream line, for better or worse, fell outside this generational description.

These men had familiar faces.

"Arabs and Persians did it first. The Persians put fruit preserves on snow, and the Arabs added milk to it. Not Romans. Not Italians. Not Nero. That came way after. In fact, Charles I of England tried to keep ice cream a secret so only the royal family could enjoy it. They didn't want to share it with the masses. They paid for that decision at the hands of the Guillotine's parents...the ax and the executioner. The people rose then. They will rise again. Thus is history!"

It was the contractor.

Neither Dewayne by his side nor the fat ice cream man in the window entertained such talk. Cameron was beginning to realize that nobody did.

"I said chocolate King Cone. Not vanilla," Dewayne said.

"I only have vanilla right now," the fat ice cream man said.

A sigh went out amongst the resident gamers. Evidently, their orders would be a disappointment as well.

When he noticed the customers' reactions, the fat ice cream man reconsidered and handed Dewayne his flavor of choice.

"I said I wanted a cup to keep it in. It's going to melt. I don't know many things, but I know that," Dewayne said.

The fat ice cream man yanked the King Cone from Dewayne's hand and squeezed it into a cup. Some of it ran in between his hairy fat fingers on its way there. When it did, the fat ice cream man shoved it back into Dewayne's face. Part of it caught his face.

"You take this cone back. Looord have mercy if you don't do it quickly," Dewayne said.

With feline quickness, the fat ice cream man lunged out from his serving window, grabbed the back of Dewayne's head and crashed it against the truck. The King Cone fell to the ground and splattered, changing a former band of smiles to a group of forlorn glances. The fat ice cream man proceeded to put Dewayne in a chokehold, tactically applied to make it seem like it was just friends fooling with each other.

Few onlookers were fooled. And those who were fooled were forced to change their minds when Dewayne, hanging in mid-air, started turning blue. At that point, the contractor motioned the fat ice cream man to release his employee.

"My friend," the fat ice cream man said to the contractor, "I've got no problem with you, but I don't want this asshole anywhere near my ice cream truck. Or, for that matter, the rest of the goons on your crew. This morning, Dewayne here pulled up to my step-daughter in a pickup and honked at her for the third day in a row when she was jogging."

"From what I heard, she put him in his place," the contractor said, grinning.

"She always does," the fat ice cream man retorted with waning anger because he found the comment funny. "What are you hiring over there anyways?"

"What's available," the contractor said. "Scholars haven't cut brick since Callicrates. But I'll talk to the crew. I assure you, it won't happen again." The contractor then took Dewayne away with his arm slung over his shoulder. As he did so, he began to explain the repercussions people used to face when one man touched another man's daughter without permission.

"'But who can discern their own errors? Forgive my hidden

faults,'" Dewayne replied as he stretched his neck in a circular motion, still within earshot of the fat ice cream man.

"Get him the fuck out of here before I tear his whole face off," the fat ice cream man yelled towards the contractor. "God help him if he comes near my daughter again and then uses that Bible-thumping bullshit to excuse himself...Next in line!" he said as he watched them fade into the distance. He turned his head back to the line and forced a smile to his face. A kid was standing below him.

This, too, was a familiar face.

"I believe you have a debt to be paid," the Scamp said. He picked up Dewayne's cone that had fallen and started eating it in one hand. In the other, he cradled a large orange water balloon.

"You've got a big mouth but no basis for that claim," the fat ice cream man said.

"No basis? You just drove away with our money ten minutes ago. What shit are you trying to pull?" the Scamp said. His teeth flared from freshly upturned lips.

"Maybe I should tell your friends here that you didn't lose their money last week," the fat ice cream man said. With that, he extended his enormous neck and head out of the window. "That's right, guys. He came down here and started bragging about how he told all of you that he lost your pizza money. Then he took that money and bought himself a nice little treat. Funny, he didn't even have enough money for what he bought, so he owed ME money. So, I took a little extra from you guys today as interest. Sue me. Looks like you got some ice cream anyways," the fat ice cream man said as he indicated Dewayne's splattered purchase in the Scamp's hand. "So, it's a win-win."

The Scamp squashed the half-eaten King Cone down on the fat ice cream man's counter.

"That's not gunna cut it. This cone was for the retarded guy you just strangled. I want another," the Scamp said.

"Get the hell out of here before I give you something worse than he got," the fat ice cream man said.

"Suit yourself," the Scamp said as he walked away.

A noise with a gentle jingle resonated through the air. Not long after that, a white truck emerged and began to circle the fat ice cream man's truck like a shark. Then the new ice cream truck came to a halt. When it did, the serving window slid open, and a cloud of tasty mist emanated from inside. Before long, though, it was gone, as the outer atmosphere swallowed the oversized refrigerator's emissions with ease. The most striking characteristic on the ice cream man behind this counter was the two-foot long ponytail that hung behind him. That defining feature aside, he stood clean and properly adorned in all the decals of his trade. He had the all-white uniform with the nametag patch sewed on in red stitching across his left breast. A rectangular hat covered the top of his head. The contrast to the unkempt fat ice cream man sitting in his shitty mini-van ice-box selling Popsicles and King Cones was staggering.

Plus, the new guy had soft serve. And the basic hierarchy of ice cream trucks tells us that a truck with no soft serve in such a scenario might as well head home.

Everyone migrated from the fat ice cream man's truck to the other truck at once.

"Pacos!" screamed the fat ice cream man. "What'd I say about coming down here?"

"Fuck you, fat man, it's a free country," the man who was presumably Pacos said.

"Yeah, for people who came through Ellis Island, not the

Rio Grande," the fat ice cream man screamed as he waved another King Cone in their direction like a saber.

"We've been in this country for ten years and have the same job as you do," said a voice that Cameron heard but couldn't see. Then he realized why the fat ice cream man had used a plural when referring to one Paco. Another face, identical in nature and wearing the same all-white uniform showed his face from behind the counter of the "Pacos" ice cream truck. The twin also had a pony tail of the same size as his brother.

Vulgarity parleyed between the trucks. Italian and Mexican epithets were served back and forth over a net of wary children.

"Pacos, I'm asking you to leave for the last time," the fat ice cream man threatened.

"You don't rule the park, fat man. We go where we please," one of the Pacos said.

"Then you won't go anywhere but underground if I get my hands on you," the fat ice cream man said. And with that, he slammed his server door and re-shifted his body perpendicular to the back of the truck to slide out. The van seesawed in that direction as he did so. First came his feet, which were inside the most gigantic pair of lime green crocs Cameron had ever seen. Then, as momentum would have it, the rest of his body followed.

After that, he began to advance towards his rivals.

Some kids caught between both parties scattered into the nearby cattails or the beach. The rest sought salvation by running towards the Pacos, who, seeing the fury of their one unwelcome and elephantine pursuer, wisely started driving in the other direction. They went at a pace that everyone could keep besides their adversary. "Run from the fat man, children," one of the Pacos urged. "He's gaining on you. If he gets here before you, they'll be no ice cream left. Hurry! Hurry!"

"Fire!" screamed the familiar high-pitched voice of the Scamp. A rubbery sting hit the fat ice cream man in the back of the head and bounced off him, splashing on the ground nearby. 'They never break on you,' the fat ice cream man said to himself, satisfied with his good fortune. Then he heard the shrieking artillery call repeated. He turned his head in its direction, opposite the Pacos. Out from behind the clump of nearby cattail brush, the Scamp emerged with a smile. His hand went up and went down. On that signal, a curtain of water balloons hijacked the ski in giant confetti fashion. All were set on the same destination – the fat ice cream man's face.

This time, quite a few broke on him.

The fat ice cream man did his best to dodge the onslaught. Given his size, that proved problematic. The kids took advantage of his state of distraction by transporting balloons across the parking lot and arming the Pacos in their truck. Now, the fat ice cream man was flanked. Balloons hit him from all sides.

In desperation, the fat ice cream man entertained his only remaining option – Bonzai attack through the firestorm and force the Pacos' truck off the premises. Despite the damage, this proved successful. The Pacos left the parking lot and drove down the road. All the children followed them, ready to buy whatever their allies had to offer.

Cameron was sitting next to the fat ice cream man's truck with his arms folded amidst the wreckage. A lot had happened fast, making it hard to track the familiar faces he'd met earlier and observe their role in the blitzkrieg. He especially watched the little boy with the heart-shaped head. During the siege of the fat ice cream man, he'd been active in the assault. Though he hadn't thrown the most balloons, those he did were delivered with deadly precision. Cameron wondered if he would have participated in this campaign at that age. If it meant gaining friends, the answer was probably yes. What they don't tell you in school is that submitting to minor peer pressures here and there is how people become friends. Throwing a couple of water balloons never hurt anyone. Good for the little boy with the heart-shaped head, Cameron thought.

The Scamp must have felt the same, because Cameron saw him patting his back in the distance. As expected, that warmth was short-lived. In a moment, the Scamp took the little boy with the heart-shaped head's hat and tossed it behind them.

"I'll have a toasted almond when you get a chance," Cameron said when the fat ice cream man returned to his truck completely drenched.

"Go fuck yourself," the fat ice cream man said as he wrung out his clothes and took off his giant lime green crocs. Red-faced, sweaty, greasy and wet, he scratched his head and breathed heavily. "And after you're done with that, you can track down the two who just left. They seem to have the ice cream of choice these days."

"I like to support local business, not big corporations. The Pacos rented that truck off some billionaire who's going to take half their profits. If I have to give my money away, it won't be to them. I also don't like pony tails," Cameron said.

"You got that right, kid. About business...and the pony tails." A smile came across his face. It was the first one he flashed since he was flooring it down the street blasting metal music. "Kids don't talk that way anymore."

"I'm just kidding. Soft serve just makes me shit. Otherwise, I'd be wailing on you with those balloons, too," Cameron said.

"That sounds more like how I thought you'd talk. Even girls speak so vulgar nowadays. You should hear the mouths on some of them my step-daughter brings around."

"It used to be Sinatra, now crude is the new cool," Cameron said.

"I like the way you think. I have a box of ice cream ready in the truck for orders that aren't happening. You want to split what's in there that hasn't melted? On me," the fat ice cream man said.

Cameron followed him to the back of the truck, trying not to laugh at the funny fart noises the massive man's wet clothes made as they rubbed against each other. The fat ice cream man opened the back door and struggled to stretch and reach for the box of cones in the freezer.

"I'll get it," Cameron said before the fat ice cream man had lodged half of his gut onto the back bumper to crawl in.

"Would ya?" the fat ice cream man said almost before Cameron asked.

When Cameron hopped into the truck, he saw a worn-out griddle against the back wall. Egg shells bordered its sides. Bacon crumbs were ingrained into the middle of the fryer. Two packages of open rolls held down by a spatula were piled on the counter.

"I sell egg sandwiches in the morning. Bad economy...you gotta do what you gotta do," the fat ice cream man said, answering the question before it came. He did so quickly so Cameron could keep his attention on retrieving the ice cream from the freezer.

They ate under the awning of the ice cream truck. Everything from Toasted Almonds and Éclairs to King Cones, even those red baseball glove shaped sorbets with the baseball bubble gum in the middle were consumed.

The fat ice cream man threw one of his wrappers to a seagull with brown spots that had just landed nearby. "So you know, I don't actually take their money. When they think I do,

I've already paid it off to their parents. It's the Pacos that I have a real problem with. For the rest of them, it's just a game we play. The fact is that most of these little shit kids have a good heart in them somewhere."

"Even the weird-looking one, your nemesis?" Cameron asked.

"Especially him," the fat ice cream man said.

"He's quite a character," Cameron said.

"You think so now, you should've seen him when he was younger before they got him some help. By them, I mean those two brothers and their family. They pretty much adopted him when his mom got sick. Been paying for his help for years now. Occupational therapy, speech therapy, social therapy, all that shit. They say he's got great potential because of how smart he is. Can't argue with that. He basically lives there. Over at their house," the fat ice cream man said.

"How do you know all that?" Cameron asked.

"Their neighbor gives me the dirt. He always buys *South of Sunrise* off me and complains about him.

"I hear that's popular stuff?" Cameron asked.

"You could say that. I'm also the only guy around here who can sell it," the fat ice cream man said.

"Why are you allowed?" Cameron asked.

The fat ice cream man tossed another wrapper in front of him to free his right hand, attracting a few more gulls in the process. Then he pointed his finger upwards to indicate the drawing on his truck, and then he told Cameron it was his own work. Back in the day, the fat ice cream man said, he dabbled in some art. He also made sure to clarify that it was just a hobby. For, to be a profession, he would have to be better, and more importantly, be paid for his work. Either way, what started as doodles to pass the time in boring grade school classes became an integral part of his lifestyle. He never left home without pen and paper. The second he saw something interesting, he stopped to sketch it.

Perhaps because at one point in his twenties he was considering transforming his hobby into a profession, the fat ice cream man joined a figure-drawing class. The class was great, but getting there was an ordeal. Besides the frustration of traveling by both trains and buses, he was always hungry before he got there and never felt like there was ample food selection in close enough proximity to where he needed to be. That is, unless he wanted to break the bank and pay high city prices. For this reason, food trucks, with their combination of big portions and small prices, became the only option to fill his stomach.

Generally, his choice at food trucks was limited to a hot dog stand or a halal truck. Every so often, though, these eateries would share space with a new curbside counterpart. On the particular day he was describing to Cameron, there happened to be an Indian food truck doing exactly that. The buzz about them, at least according to their sign, was their beef kati rolls. A plain eater in most circumstances, he decided to give this brand of ethnic food a go. After he scarfed them down, he decided that they were not his favorite but made a mental note that they were satisfying enough to be ordered in the future. With that, he headed to his destination, the figure-drawing class.

The nude model in the studio that day was a pleasure to draw. Her symmetry, her curves, her joint structure, from her jaw to her elbows to her knees and all the way down to the arches of her ankles and the spaces between her toes, all of it was flawless. This, added to the drawing, the fraternizing, and the sharing of a bottle of Merlot, made for a slice of paradise thicker than the last piece of cheese the future fat ice cream man swallowed from a platter he took too much of.

Unfortunately, it did not take long for his belly to churn and gurgle. This put the fat ice cream man in a predicament. Since the future fat ice cream man had drained enough glasses of wine and had chomped on enough blocks of cheese in his day without issue, he was convinced it was the damn Indian food that was responsible. The solution to his problem was probably a rather lengthy and uncomfortable defecation session in the nearest restroom. That solution, though, would make him miss the rest of the beautiful woman posing. As a result, he fended off his bowels, spreading his cheeks and discharging his flatulence in silence. The smell was noxious, but because people were close by, he believed he was safe from blame. He glanced around the room to see if he noticed anything that would warrant reconsideration of that notion. A few other men in the group and one, maybe two women, were potential scapegoats. That would put him in the clear.

Hopes of anonymity were short-lived. One woman was discrete about it but nonetheless left the room. Another woman followed, coughing and holding her nose under her shirt. The two other guys looked at each other and agreed that the stench was far too awful to stay in the room. The few remaining women had no choice when the men were gone. It was leave or risk unjustified humiliation.

Soon, it was just the future fat ice cream man and the nude model in the room. A true professional, she continued to hold her pose and did so with a smile despite her evident difficulty breathing.

"Excuse me," she said to the future fat ice cream man. "I am really sorry."

"For what?" the future fat ice cream man asked, readying himself for a shaming.

"It's just that it's not my fault. I had some rotten Indian food. That's all. It was from a truck down the road," the beautiful woman said.

"Oh, I don't mind. I know how you feel," the future fat ice cream man replied, relieved.

Not long after that, they were hitched. The honeymoon that followed was not your typical island getaway. The future fat ice cream man loved history, Civil War history in particular. William T. Sherman's "March to the Sea" was what he found most interesting within that context. In the eyes of the fat ice cream man, Sherman's scorched earth policy was one of the main reasons the Union Army won the war. Without it, a different flag may be hanging from the White House lawn. For that reason, he always believed we needed more Shermans. Yet, with the passage of time and the more he looked, the less he saw them.

If pressed, the beautiful woman would have said that William T. Sherman was a barbarian. A man who could turn half of his country to ash was no less a devil than a red monster with horns and a tail that was holding a pitchfork. But at the moment of their honeymoon, that was neither here nor there. The beautiful woman was happy with the fact that she finally found someone she felt safe and comfortable being herself around. Years had been spent doing two things: trying to mask her imperfections for work and battling with men who just couldn't control themselves at home. If the fat ice cream man's major flaw was worshipping a general from a century ago who killed a lot of people for the sake of the greater good, she could live with that. She knew from experience there were worse things.

So, they hopped on a plane destined for a honeymoon that began in Vicksburg, Mississippi, a starting point that was a no-brainer to the future fat ice cream man. According to him, Vicksburg was where Sherman started to become Sherman. So, after a night was spent in the casinos, the real trip began. An RV was rented. A course of Sherman's victories heading back east was charted. The engine revved. And off they went.

From Vicksburg, they cut across to Tennessee to see the historical landmark for the Battle of Missionary Ridge. Next, they journeyed deep into Dixie, burning rubber the way Sherman burnt every blade of grass from Atlanta to its most infamous port city in Savannah. Somewhere between these places, on some quaint dirt road outside of time, there was a peach farm protected by a cattle fence where an old man was selling produce. Suddenly, they were hungry.

They pulled over. The old man selling produce's wife had been standing on the other side of the table when they did so. She said hello. Then she took a walk down the road. She pushed a cooler with wheels along the way. Apparently, she was inquiring whether her workers were thirsty.

"Neither good fruits nor good looking woman last long by the roadside. African proverb," the future fat ice cream man said to the man selling produce.

"That's why we have the Second Amendment," the old man selling produce said. They had a good laugh about that. He also said his .22 in his truck was as much his baby as his little girls, who were probably about fifty or so at the time. Age didn't matter, though. In the South, you're always someone's little girl until you're six feet under. Hearing the words "little girl" made the future fat ice cream man grab his wife's hand and tell the old man selling produce that they had a little girl on the way themselves. 'Look at that beautiful wife of yours,' the old man selling produce said. Then he got up from behind the table and asked the future fat ice cream man for permission to dance with his wife. When he approved, the old man selling produce did a little celebratory jig with the beautiful woman. His rhythm and grace was of someone half his age.

The sun was hot, and the peaches were soft. Many had already fallen victim to insects and the elements. All of these concerns made the man selling produce leave his dance partner and return back to business. He offered the couple a simple menu. Georgia peaches: fresh, rotten or unripe. The decision of what to buy was even simpler. But out of respect, the couple pretended to make the process more difficult than it actually was. During the selection process, the man selling produce returned to his wooden rocking chair and gulped down a glass of orange liquid. Then he lit a pipe and grabbed a large knife. With the knife, he scraped some peach guts off the checkered tablecloth in front of him. They landed in a bowl on his lap.

After careful deliberation, as well as some insistence from the man selling produce, they ended up ordering samples of the whole menu.

When they were finished with the peaches, they asked where they should dispose of their used napkins. The old man selling produce told them to leave them on the table and he'd attend to them later. If their hands were sticky, he said they could rinse off in the bucket in the shade up yonder. He didn't offer any particular direction as to where this bucket was, or where yonder meant, a trait they found consistent throughout all their ventures in the region. Everyone just expected everyone else to know where the thing was that they were talking about. If experience told them anything, however, it was that the word 'yonder' usually didn't mean too close. Not to mention, "close," to country folks, was a measure based on its own odometer. So, they declined the old man's gestures towards yonder, assuring him they had wipes in the car and would wash up as soon as they were back inside. After that, they said their goodbyes, the future fat ice cream man and his beautiful wife insisting all the while that the old man selling produce give their best to his wife upon her return.

Due to the urging of his wife, the future fat ice cream man also left a hearty tip for the old man selling produce. Since there was a breeze, he wrapped the tip in a napkin and put a peach on top of it. He included his contact information on the napkin and told the old man selling produce to never hesitate to reach out if he ever went North. The old man selling produce said that he wouldn't be going up North unless there was another war to fight. They had a good laugh over that.

The future fat ice cream man left the napkin anyway. He did so because on the unexposed side of the napkin, he had drawn the old man selling produce dancing with his wife. The sketch also contained a table with peaches and a quick fence with some overhanging peach trees. Behind that, if you looked closely enough in between those trees, one could just make out the rear end of the old man selling produce's wife. Her butt was sticking out towards the road as she peered through the cattle fence into the farm trying to tend to her workers.

Not too long after, they were home from their honeymoon, and in their new house did the future fat ice cream man receive a package at the door. In a brown box addressed to him and 'that beautiful wife of yours' was a pallet of that orange drink the man selling produce had been slugging down. It was a type of fruity semi-carbonated soft drink, not smooth enough to be juice or syrupy enough to be soda. The label on the glass bottle was a familiar image: it was the sketch on the napkin. When the future fat ice cream man popped a glass open and took a sip, he tasted money in a bottle. Next thing he knew, he was on the phone trying to convince the old man selling produce of the drink's potential. For years, the courting process would continue. Nevertheless, the man selling produce was a prideful Southerner forever skeptical of big business. No matter what he wanted, he wanted his drink to remain a small-town concoction, available only to the local folk and the occasional honeymooning wanderers.

A decade passed in the life of the future fat ice cream man. Like clockwork, once a year, always at the start of summer, a pallet of bottles was delivered to the fat ice cream man's doorstep. When the old man selling produce died one winter, the future fat ice cream man believed he would have to part with this traditional gift. But low and behold, the bottles kept coming that summer as they always had. It didn't take long to realize that the old man selling produce's daughters were behind the gesture. It also didn't take long to realize they had better business minds than their father. With limited convincing, the fat ice cream man was permitted to sell *South of Sunrise*. And, as expected, customers loved the drink the second it started selling out of his truck.

"If you want to grab some, there's a couple in the cooler in the back of the truck to the left of the King Cones," the fat ice cream man said.

Cameron went into the truck again and grabbed two glass bottles of *South of Sunrise*. There it was – an orange drink with a label that depicted an old man dancing with a beautiful young woman in front of a table full of peaches. The image left no doubt that this label was the work of the same artist who painted the fat ice cream man on the truck.

When Cameron came out with the drinks, they said cheers. Then they clanged glasses and started drinking.

"What were we talking about before I went on that tangent?" the fat ice cream man asked Cameron while taking quite the satisfying gulp of *South of Sunrise.*

"The neighbor to those boys," Cameron said.

"Oh yeah, that's right. He's a nice fellow. A bit strange, though. His wife left him and took the kids across the country. Ever since, he's been hard on the kids next door. I don't think his mother getting sick helped the matter much either," the fat ice cream man said. "I didn't think we were talking about him, though. I think we were talking about those damn Pacos."

"Aren't you being a bit juvenile with this whole Pacos thing?" Cameron asked.

"My income depends on dominating this area. I have to do all I can to keep it," the fat ice cream man said. "I'm up against corporate monsters here, kid. Those ice cream trucks that the Pacos drive are everywhere. They can charge half what I can and make a better product. How do I compete with that?" he asked. "And to top it off, compared to my refurbished minivan here, they might as well be driving around in Lamborghinis."

"You could join them?" Cameron suggested as he pondered the question himself.

"I don't live by anyone else's rules anymore. I'm independent. My own man," the fat ice cream man said.

Cameron asked him about what he did before the ice cream truck. All the fat man said was that there were parts of business that couldn't be taught in a classroom. Those were the things he was involved in.

"Where does the ice cream truck fit in?" Cameron asked.

"In September 2008, the financial crisis hit. When it did, I saw it as a time for a new beginning. So, I asked myself, 'what do people like more than anything when they're depressed?'"

"Ice cream," Cameron said.

The fat ice cream man nodded.

"Soft serve," Cameron added.

"Fuck yourself," the fat ice cream man said as he undid the golden wrapping of another King Cone and threw it at the birds. "Those fucking Mexican bastards and their corporate sponsors and their goddamned soft-serve mother fucking ice cream." He squeezed the cone in his hand until the pressure gave way and ice cream spewed out from the middle of the wafer.

"So, how can you compete with them?" Cameron asked.

"I can't," the fat ice cream man said.

"So, what will you do?" Cameron asked.

"I lose sleep over that question every night," the fat ice cream man said. "I don't want to go back to my old ways."

"You're a smart guy. I can tell. You'll find something. You were on the pulse with ice cream in 2008. People definitely needed a cone then. Maybe you should just take that concept and apply it to another more relevant idea," Cameron said.

The fat ice cream man let out a long sigh and looked towards the sky. A hawk was flying high above them. "I see that hawk circling above me all the time, and I can't help but think it senses that I'm dying down here," he said.

"Maybe, but the seagulls down here think you're a god. You've given them a feast," Cameron said. "It's all perspective."

By now, there must have been ten seagulls fighting for the King Cone wrappers the fat ice cream man had thrown away. Some sparrows joined in on the action, too. They did so at the risk of being swatted or stomped out by a bigger species of bird. Speaking of birds, behind them a crow sat on a telephone wire scoffing at the stupidity of the whole scene.

"When I see all of this it makes me wonder whether Darwin and Wallace were just brave men willing to state the obvious,"

Cameron said. Then he patted the fat ice cream man on the back and looked at the box still glued between his legs. Only two cones were left. The fat ice cream man went for one of them but reconsidered midway down. He clapped his hands and rubbed them together. "No more for me. You take them," he said to Cameron.

"Why's that?" Cameron asked.

"I've got to get going. Birds aren't the only species that have to figure out how to evolve," the fat ice cream man said.

7

A Libation at the Altar of the Average Joe

Cameron left the ice cream truck duel-fisting two cones. While walking back towards the Old Shoaling Road, he saw a young woman leaned against the railing of the dock facing the water. Her gaze onto the horizon was pensive and penetrating, giving the impression that it was her, rather than the passing boats, that caused the nearby waves to wake. It was a posture Cameron associated with a person bent over a good book, though in this case, the book was intangible, printed across cumulus clouds and catalogued within the infinite library of the sky.

Cameron approached her. The old wooden dock whined beneath his feet when he did so. This caught her attention. She turned towards him. In moving, she revealed two stoplight green eyes, pairs of which are more native to felines inhabiting dark alleyways than on modern Aphrodites.

"Looking for something?" he asked her. He hoped such a dull inquiry could spawn conversation.

"Aren't we all?" she replied as she took off a hairband from around her wrist to tie back her golden mane. It was long and blonde and billowed in the wind as the waves she watched did in the water.

"I wasn't expecting such a philosophical response to that question," Cameron smiled uncomfortably.

"And why is that, do I look stupid?" she said.

"Sorry, I didn't mean to..." Cameron said.

"Relax," she said. "I was just kidding."

As she said this, she bent down to look under a bench in the middle of the dock. Her cutoff T-shirt was the type that allowed for the slightest glimpse down her shirt. Transfixed on her chest, he didn't even realize what the young beautiful woman was doing down there. It turned out that there was a dog under the bench and she had taken it upon herself to fish him out. When the animal finally complied with her wishes, it rolled over. Apparently, it was intent on a belly rub in exchange for its obedience. That demand was fulfilled. The young beautiful woman bent down and did just that. In the process, she revealed to Cameron another piece of eye candy. Right beneath her lumbar spine, moist from sweat and covered with an ever so slight amount of blonde peach fuzz when it caught the sun, was a tattoo. The tattoo depicted the tip of a Viking ship moving forward in stormy seas. A mermaid was carved into the front of its bow.

"Is it hard to be beautiful?" Cameron asked.

"I can think of other types of adversity that are harder to overcome, but it has its difficulties," she said.

"I was talking to the dog," Cameron said.

She laughed. They both laughed.

"Such a dad joke," she said.

"Is that a good thing?" Cameron asked.

"I don't know. I'm more familiar with grandfather jokes. He

was the male figure around me when I was growing up," she said.

"Why?" Cameron asked.

"My dad was always at work. He did math stuff on Wall Street," she said.

"So, you got close to your grandfather in your father's absence?" Cameron asked.

"The only person who was closer was his wife. Other than that, I'm the favorite," she said.

"Why's that?" Cameron asked.

"I think because I like to listen to what he had to say. Not a lot of people are good at that. And he told great stories. I learned a lot from him," she said.

"Like what?" Cameron asked.

"That all of us have talents. Life is about finding out what those talents are and using them the right way to get the most out of life," she said.

"Is your gift like your dad's? Are you a math whiz?" Cameron asked.

"Not like he is," she said.

"So, I guess that means you don't do that kind of work," Cameron asked.

"God, no," she said. "When I'm not here as a lifeguard, I'm a waitress."

Cameron felt uneasy when women said they worked jobs like waitressing. That is not to say that he had objections to the job. In fact, he believed it was a great way to harness social grace and learn how to work hard. In high school, he even wanted to be one for a while, but that fell through because he was too afraid of the human interaction, especially in cases involving importunate fat people demanding special sauces. But to him, it always seemed like the person who said they worked as a waitress was preprogrammed to call him a snob no matter how he responded.

"I'd imagine you're also in school?" Cameron asked.

"Why do you say that?" she asked.

"You seem too smart to..." Cameron said.

"Be a waitress?" she asked.

"I didn't mean it like that," Cameron said.

"Look, I'm young and in my prime; I make great money, I do everything I want to do, I don't have much pressure. I know what people say behind my back. But the reality is that I've lived, I've traveled, I've met loads of great people, and I've done it independently. My debt will be low, and I can spend my 30's rather than my 20's wasting away in the library. I'll be losing my looks by that time anyways, right?" she smiled at him. "Plus, all of my friends with degrees are back from college, and guess what? They're all taking orders from me because they needed jobs at the restaurant after all that school. What is it you do anyway?"

Cameron was jealous. He felt that this woman had the guts to live life the way he wanted to but didn't.

"Here, have a King Cone," Cameron said, "You deserve it."

She laughed and took the cone out of his hand and fed it to the dog named Lionheart.

"I guess you're a nutrition freak then? I could have guessed," Cameron said. "No need to inquire. I am, too. I actually wasn't going to eat this one either."

"I eat junk. I just don't take candy from strangers," she said.

"Yes, you do, you just give it to the dog," Cameron said.

"Good point. Normally, I'd take it, I swear. I could never live by a strict diet. Not sustainable. Plus, I don't know why anyone would spend their life torturing themselves and avoiding pleasure by choice. We don't live long enough for that type of radicalism. What the hell makes somebody happier in life than ice cream anyways? A good body? You can have it."

Cameron wanted to note how it was easy for her to say such a thing given the fact that she could have been Botticelli's inspiration for the "re-birth of Venus." He also wanted to say that there was a good possibility this would change as her beauty clock continued to tick. The men who worshipped her now would be less inclined to kiss the ring when their golden calf began to rust. Slowly and at first unnoticeably, men would stop holding doors for her, letting her into parking spots, highway lanes, lines at bagel shops, cafes, and fast food drive-throughs. In time, she'd come to terms with this, let herself go and settle for a cheap mold of what her former self would've tolerated as a partner. Far too many little kids would follow to make up for this. Inevitably, they'd suck her dry in the teat then do the same to her wallet.

But maybe he was being too hard on her. After all, he knew deep down they all weren't the same, beautiful women that is, and he hardly knew enough of them to make the generalization even if it was true.

"So then, why not the cone?" he asked.

"I feel like all I've eaten lately is junk food. I've been binging because I just broke up with my boyfriend," she said.

"What kind of dog is he?" Cameron asked after a pause. He changed the subject because he was too uncomfortable to press the boyfriend issue or muster the courage to ask her out.

"Lionheart? Funny you ask that. I found the answer to that question today," she said.

That morning, while sitting atop the lifeguard stand, she watched a man in teeny European swim briefs go through a half-hour Tai Chi routine. To warm up, he bounced on his toes and swung his neck from side to side. Next, he moved both of his hands around an imaginary beach ball in front of his face. While transitioning to another posture, a dog charged him and knocked him over. After a moment of shellshock, the man regained his composure and readied himself for another bludgeoning. The young beautiful woman ran over, terrified, because she thought it was real, that the dog was readying to maul him. Such a belief was further supported when the man and the beast went to the floor on top of one another. Not until she was nearly on the pile herself did she realize these antics were of the playful variety. Once that was clear, she struck up a conversation with the man. This led to the answer about the dog.

"He was a nice guy," she said to Cameron. "A bit odd, though. He kept relating everything to history. He said that the wrestling he was doing with Lionheart was how the ancient Lydians trained their separate dog battalions for war in 628 B.C."

"That sounds about right," Cameron said of her description. "Why is he named Lionheart?"

"Do you know anything about Rhodesian Ridgebacks?" she asked.

"Nope," Cameron said as he crouched to eye level with Lionheart and patted his head.

It was no wonder why the contractor had taken a liking to the dog. Aside from the hairy ridge protruding down the spinal column, every inch of Lionheart's body was rock. Only his fur prevented one from thinking he'd been plucked off the pillar of an old mansion. Well, that and the fact that gargoyles weren't as appreciative of a good belly rub. When Lionheart rolled over and demanded one then and there, the dog revealed a chest cavity so dense and finely barreled that evolution could be called a cooper. The sternum, the house of Lionheart's life force, was a secured fortress well-protected against anything short of a brutal blow.

"Rhodesians were bred in South Africa to hunt lions," she said. "Their job was to track a cat through the savanna and tangle with it until a hunter caught up and finished the job."

"And if the hunter was too far behind?" Cameron asked.

"There are always other dogs," she said.

"As there are hunters," Cameron said. "I guess that's how he got his name?" he asked.

She nodded as she bent down and cupped Lionheart's cheeks in her hands. She spoke to the animal in that customary high-pitched baby voice that people use to communicate with their pets. The dog soaked it up in a way that made Cameron wonder if the animal knew Cameron would have preferred the treatment it was receiving from the beautiful woman.

"I do love him. But he isn't mine. He's a neighborhood stray that everybody loves and kind of collectively takes care of," she said.

For better or worse, Lionheart was a rover, a rover born and raised on the streets and there destined to remain, surviving on puddles and pond water, the town's all too frequent leftovers, and freedom.

Despite being a vagabond, in the summer the faintest bark awarded him swimming pool privileges. In the winter, a gentle scratch on a door gave him a place at the fireside of his choosing. For food, there was always a leftover to be offered. And if for some reason that became unavailable, the fishermen reserved some spare catch for him on their way back from the docks.

Cameron looked at the animal, this suburban Huckleberry Finn on four legs. Then he said, "Funny how a dog could live like a king and still be such a tramp."

"Don't call him that," she asked politely but sternly.

"What's the big deal, it's not a bad word, you know, at least to me. I don't buy into that whole double standard bullshit about men being able to sleep with as many people as they want and women having to be selective or regarded as sluts. We're so afraid of sexuality in this country. Kudos to the slut. They give the establishment the finger and say, judge me if you want, you hypocrites, but I'm going to act like everyone else does."

"There's more to it than just hypocrisy and patriarchal values that create the double standard," the young beautiful woman said.

"What's the other part of it?" Cameron asked.

"Men don't care about being pigs and women do," she said.

He had never thought of it that way.

Cameron got up from petting the dog on the stomach. The animal was taking a liking to him, which was fine now that the seafood stench of the Rhodesian's breath was being overpowered by the beautiful woman's pleasant scent. Cameron could not specifically identify her fragrance, but he knew it reminded him of arboretum greenhouses in the winter. He needed that quick fix of summer and the exotic to get him through the dark months. And by dark months, he meant much more than just the weather. He took another deep sniff, as deep as he could without making it obvious what his nose was after. Oh, what it'd be like, he wondered, to wake up next to a woman like this who offered so much springtime no matter the season.

Once he regained his composure, Cameron felt he had overstayed his welcome. He did, however, have an inkling that she wanted to keep talking. The normal signs were there. She touched his arm when she spoke, she maintained eye contact, she smiled when she spoke. Yet Cameron believed, as he often did, that the connection was more of an audience/entertainer relationship than it was two individuals interacting as equals. In other words, he was the clown on stage, sore from squeaking his red nose, wet from the water in his flower boutonniere, blistered from tying too many balloon animals and fully knowledgeable that he was battling his audience and time. A typical 10 p.m. special. That's what he came to call his dealings with women. Prep them early in the evening. Give them their laughs and their intellectual stimulation. Then, when substance was satisfied, off they go. Bound, no doubt, to exchange late night passions with more desirable men.

This circulated in his mind during the whole conversation and convinced him to decide against asking for her number. He believed this would bother her for a number of reasons. For one, she would not get the satisfaction of denying him as a suitor, a pleasure he oddly believed she'd care about; and two, she'd be forced to recognize there were rogue men out there, who she considered below her, that could find her disinteresting. If not for anything else, his sacrifice would be a libation placed at the altar of the Average Joe.

"Well, I better be going," Cameron said.

She laughed and shook her head in agreement. "Yeah, me too." The young beautiful woman turned towards the lifeguard stand. A brief silence followed when she turned back again, at which point, they just looked at each other. Even so, Cameron kept his mouth shut. Now, though, he was forced to face the truth. He refrained from asking her out due to cowardice, not because he cared one way or another for the average Joe.

So, they said their goodbyes, and to the discomfort of both, walked off side-by-side in the same direction. Cameron slowed his pace so this could discontinue. When she got ahead of him, he backpedaled to the dock railing and leaned his back against it. Intent on one last look, his eyes trailed her until her body began to blur next to what appeared to be her car.

She started to pack her trunk and get ready to leave. In the process of doing so, she pulled out a pair of grey dress pants and a black dress shirt. As for her footwear, given what was now being placed on the tailgate, it seemed like her flip flops would soon be substituted for heels.

"That doesn't look like a typical waitressing outfit," Cameron said.

"That's because it isn't a waitressing outfit," she said. "I took the night off."

"Big party somewhere?" Cameron asked, trying to act indifferent, as indifference for some reason is considered cool.

"I suppose," she said.

"You look nice," he said.

"Thanks," she said as she smiled and entered her car.

He took a deep breath. His face flushed. His heart was beating fast.

"I want your phone number," Cameron said before she could close her window and back out.

He was so proud of himself.

"Sure," she said. Then she wrote the information he requested on a ketchup-stained napkin laying on the passenger seat.

"How about a ride to go with that?" Cameron asked.

"Don't push it," she said smiling.

And then she sped off.

8

A Life Jacket and a Bottle of Booze

A burgundy Dodge Dart fresh off the lot zoomed into the middle of two parking spaces and slammed on the brakes. The wheels screeched. Both back tires left a rubbery residue to mark where they once were. Cameron came to two conclusions. The driver had neither command nor respect for his vehicle.

Since everyone with a nice car likes to be told they have a nice car, Cameron went to praise the driver. At the same time, he wanted to see if the driver was as much a dick as the way he drove, which was usually the case. Inside the Dart, a man dressed as a middle-aged professional was pounding a 24 oz Pabst Blue Ribbon. When that beer was done being pounded, the man with the beers rolled down his window and threw the 24 oz towards the trash bin in front of his car. It fell short of the can by a few feet. Bothered by the piggery and the environmental disregard, Cameron went over and put the trash where it belonged.

As Cameron did this, his back was turned away from the Dart. That was when he felt something cold and sticky hit him and run down his back. Alas, it was another 24 oz can of Pabst Blue Ribbon, this time disposed of a bit unfinished.

Cameron turned his head to look at the man with the beers again.

"What the fuck are you looking at?" the man with the beers said.

Cameron smiled. At this point in the day, he had grown accustomed to unconventional greetings.

"You left a little bit," Cameron said to him as he shook the can.

"I don't drink the ass," the man with the beers said, barely paying attention to him. "Unless I get a good price," he said with a wry smile. From the jumbled articulation of his words, he was clearly intoxicated.

"That's where we're different," Cameron said. And he drank the remaining liquid rattling in the bottom of the can, fountaining the remains in a two-foot stream from his elevated hand to his mouth and then swallowing. To celebrate finishing, Cameron did a weird little dance. As much as the man with the beers tried not to smile, he snorted and burst out laughing.

"You're a crazy son of a bitch. I like that...here, have a full one. On me," the man with the beers said. Then he tossed another 24 oz can of Pabst in Cameron's direction.

"Good hands," the man with the beers said.

"You know it. Cool car," Cameron said.

The man with the beers took another swig and swung open the passenger side door with his leg and motioned Cameron to sit next to him. For a second, Cameron thought of everything he'd learned about not getting in the car with strangers or taking things they offered as a coaxing device. Then he realized that the door would remain open and that, given he was an adult, he was not the intended audience for such words of caution.

The man with the beers must have sensed his discomfort, so he said, "Usually, candy is the way to seduce people. I guess when they get older, it's better to try beers." They both laughed.

"You know, you shouldn't drink and drive," Cameron said.

"Cheers to that," the man with beers said. They slammed their cans together and drank.

Cameron spun the PBR can in his hand. Then he read the words imprinted on the cylindrical piece of aluminum. "Established in Milwaukee 1844."

The man with the beers responded with a diatribe about how Captain Pabst, the founder of the company, was an ideal American.

"Why was he called a Captain?" Cameron asked.

"He was a captain of a ship. That is, until he got shipwrecked on Lake Michigan and decided after some soul searching that it was time for a new profession. The company started soon after. Here's to him." They agreed to cheers as he said this.

"It took a shipwreck for him to realize he needed to change his life?" Cameron asked.

"Shipwrecks happen to everyone, kid, I guarantee you that," the man with the beers said. For the first time, he was serious. "Here's to him!" Again, they brought their cans together for cheers.

"Seems nowadays fewer people are able to escape being marooned," Cameron said.

"Well, no one is shipwrecked with the same stuff. So, I'm not sure if it's fair to judge a man who shows up on a raft after a shipwreck the same way you judge a man who floated in on a yacht," the man with the beers said.

"What did you show up on?" Cameron asked.

"A life jacket and a bottle of booze," the man with the beers said.

"That was enough?" Cameron asked.

"Back then it was," the man with the beers said. Then he looked at Cameron and shared a story about his younger days as an electrical engineer. Not an electrical engineer in the sense that he had a degree, but in the sense of how the term was used years ago, when a title was acquired on merit, not educational degree.

"In those days, you showed up at an interview, proved you had the potential to do the job, and you were working the next day. The promise of a good salary capable of supporting a family of whatever size was the norm, not the exception. None of this resume bullshit mattered, you know, where you craft everything you've ever done on a piece of paper and fine tune it by having specialists tell you what is important about your life. But Archie Bunker's dead, kid, and so too is that way of life."

"He's so dead, I don't even know who you're talking about," Cameron said.

"My point exactly," the man with the beers said.

"Where did you work?" Cameron asked.

"All over, but most importantly in Canada," the man with the beers said.

The man with the beers was in Canada because the project he was working on was so successful domestically that the Canadian government sought their services across the border. Contracts were therefore signed right after ground broke in Maine. Just like that, the new endpoint changed from a spot one hundred miles north of Augusta to a location deep in the thick of the Canadian tundra. Somewhere in those parts, a tower had been erected to bring technology to the area. Their job was to give that tower life.

But problems arose en route to the tower. Among other things, fellow workers in the man with the beers' group began to flee. To stay, they said, was insanity, which was all the more true because the Canadian winter was coming, and it would be weeks before they even reached the tower.

Common sense said to leave. The job was bad pay, and the economy was good enough back home where working in such conditions was stupid. On top of that, the workers had acquired highly desirable skillsets from their work up to this point to get other jobs. Those recent developments could be credited to their newly naturalized boss, Ivan Slitzenokov. The man taught them things that would take a lifetime to learn outside the presence of such a great mind. Nevertheless, as soon as other opportunities arrived, they gave thanks with a slap on the back and a see you later and were on their way. In no time, a team of twenty was a team of two. This included team lead Ivan Slitzenokov and the man with the beers.

It was a peculiar pairing. Both had complained more along the United States campaign than anyone who'd left, both gave better arguments for leaving than any dissenters, both hated the job more than anyone, both, especially Ivan Slitzenokov, fought with upper-management about increased workers' rights...but both remained. Along with their groans and their tools, they were both ingrained with a certain stubbornness that would see them to the grave before they left a project incomplete. Ivan Slitzenokov attributed this to his Russian upbringing. What also could be attributed to his Russian upbringing was his Russian bias. For instance, in Ivan

Slitzenokov's mind, there was no winter like a Russian winter. To complain in Canada, then, would show weakness, or worse, evidentiary proof that he was not tough enough to last in his native country.

References to Russia were not limited to the winter, however. In fact, much of what Ivan Slitzenokov said concerned the greatness of his homeland. To prove this point, he selected some stories more frequently than others. His most impassioned diatribes or stories, perhaps even lectures, the man with the beers was unsure what to call them really, surrounded Napoleon's march on, and subsequent departure from, Moscow. As could be predicted, Ivan Slitzenokov dedicated more time to the French Emperor fleeing the city he burned than on actually burning it.

To Ivan Slitzenokov, everything came down to September 7, 1812. That was the date of the Battle of Borodino, the bloodiest single-day military exchange during the French invasion of Russia. Ivan Slitzenokov, never a man to think in black and white, cleverly called Borodino a loss resulting in victory. He said that even though the French advanced after Borodino, the French Grande Armee also started to bleed from a wound healable only by amputation, amputation in the form of an exodus from the Russian homeland. What he loved about it, and he couldn't help continually thanking Leo Tolstoy for this realization, was the contradiction between the two armies that ultimately led to their fate. Enter the French, a standardized, industrious, enlightened, almost global, military machine – the model for wars to come. Then consider the Russians, a haggard band of soldiers and mishmash militia inspired to defend their homeland from an enemy who appeared to have God incarnate as their leader. Such emotions gave the Russians just enough of an advantage to ultimately vanquish their foe back across (and beneath) the ice of the Berezina River and out of their country. In the wake of this awful scene, Napoleon, who Ivan Slitzenokov mockingly called 'the little man king', could not be found. For he had fled like a coward and left his men for the water, the ice, or certain slaughter. "God or not," Ivan Slitzenokov would say, "in Russia, we would've hung him first and tried him second for that."

All in all, Ivan Slitzenokov saw Borodino as a microcosm of the contradictions of life. He taught the man with the beers that sometimes we have to be French, and other times we need to be Russian.

"Seems like you learned a lot about each other?" Cameron said to the man with the beers.

"Sometimes, I wish I learned as much about my wife," the man with the beers joked, even though there seemed to be some sincerity in his voice. "Ivan Slitzenokov and I didn't really have much of a choice, though. I mean, we were the only people out there by the tower. In cases like that, you learn to tolerate what you have. Eventually, you realize people are people. They laugh, they cry and they get cold."

The man with the beers took another beer out before continuing. It was the last beer. When the man with the beers realized this, he offered to split it with Cameron. Cameron declined, but the man with the beers wouldn't take no for an answer. So, he opened and poured half of the beverage into a coffee mug that was in his cup holder. What was left in the can he gave to Cameron. When this was done, they both resumed their drinking.

"Kid, I don't know how anything survives anywhere near that place." He shook his head, returning to the memory. "There were days I'd be using a saw to cut some pipes, you know, to snake wires through, and I'd have to routinely check whether I chopped off a finger…or worse. And it was so dark that an already hard job was made that much harder. For five months, I ate all of my meals accompanied by artificial light. I never saw the spring quarter up there, or summer for that matter. Too bad, I consider myself a fair person and judging a place solely on its most brutal seasons doesn't seem right," the man with the beers said.

"So, go back," Cameron said.

"Times aren't easy, kid. I don't have the luxury to go international traveling," the man with the beers said.

"It's only international traveling because of semantics. Truth is, you can take a bus up there for sixty bucks. It won't be luxurious, but you'll get there," Cameron said.

He took a moment to contemplate what Cameron said. Then he went back to talking about his Canadian expedition.

One particular night, work demanded Ivan Slitzenokov and the man with the beers to climb the icy metal step ladder to the top of the tower spire. Despite the subfreezing temperatures, at some point, they did ascend to their intended destination point, and at some point, the work, harrowing as it was, got done. When it did, both men took a seat atop the tower to a tune of two sighs of relief. The spot they chose allowed their feet to hang over a ledge so steep it would force a bird to exercise caution. However, dangerous as it was, the panoramic view of the countryside was nothing short of spectacular. To the south, the blackness was speckled with light like fireflies that really were cities afar. To the north was the unforgiving tundra, a barren treeless wilderness where only beasts who evolved to take on torture could barter with nature to exist. If it was calm, it was calm like a graveyard. Yes, nature's true graveyard. The life that remained here despite this fact contained itself within a scattered batch of lonely plants on the not too distant horizon.

Little did the rest of the world know, these last vestiges of life inherited the grandiose responsibility of maintaining this glacial valley of the kings.

Ivan Slitzenokov cleared his throat of the phlegm that had been bothering him since the start of the job.

"You know those little shrubs out there?" said Ivan Slitzenokov.

"Sure," said the man with the beers.

"Those shitty little shrubs live where the mightiest of trees would die," Ivan Slitzenokov said.

Since the night of that conversation, the man with the beers wanted to dig up one of those shrubs and give it to Ivan Slitzenokov as a parting gift. On the night they officially finished their project, he decided to pursue that objective. The shrub he sought was rooted in a small patch of vegetation that crept over a teacup gulley one hundred yards north of the tower. He went about the task alone, with nothing but his person and a spade to uproot his prize. Ivan Slitzenokov was already asleep, passed out from a celebratory drunk dedicated to a job well done.

When the man with the beers was within a few yards of the shrub, he removed his snowshoes. He did this because he needed his boots. Snowshoes could not be used to wield a spade. Nevertheless, the digging process was short-lived. After only a few shovels, the man with the beers lost his footing in a tiny burrow hole. By the time his downward plunge concluded, his feet were well below the snow floor. At first, this fact seemed trivial. That is, until the man with the beers went to move his feet and realized he couldn't move. A quick assessment of the situation made him confident that they were lodged into something below. With some additional effort and some altering in technique, he managed to get one foot free. Unfortunately, the boot for that foot remained lodged where it was, as did the sock still tightly balled up inside of it. The other foot stayed stuck, also with its boot in place.

He screamed at himself for the stupidity of all of this. Then he cursed everything, his life, Ivan Slitzenokov, the snowshoes he stupidly took off, his boots and his shovel. Wait, he thought. The shovel.

He immediately grabbed the cursed now beloved tool and started flinging the snow from his body, every part of which was numbing fast, especially the exposed bare foot.

Five minutes of digging reinvigorated his body and generated some temporary and much-needed heat. Hope, man's prize fighter against calamity, also played a factor, when the man with the beers saw that the snow moved easier than expected. Soon his boots, wedged in between a collection of jagged rocks, were visible. With the help of both hands and less snow to keep them stuck, the man with the beers managed to dislodge both feet. Only the boot was still stuck. Feeling strong from this accomplishment and the newfound freedom it brought, the man with the beers was drawn back to the shrub, which now had an exposed root ball. As if it were destiny, in his efforts to free his feet, the man with the beers had finished most of the job he had set here to do on the shrub. All that was left was a little extra digging beneath the root ball. That would sever the remaining few root stragglers.

So, bitter with cold, with every piece of his body frozen save his mind, the man with the beers ordered his extremities to grab the shovel and start digging again, this time not at the snow but at the last remaining frozen ground around the circumference of the shrub. The first few attempts at the soil and the root ball came easy. Just a few more shots at each corner of the root ball would do it. Three more...two more...one more.

A rush of adrenaline filled his veins. Huddled in his hole, feelings of strength overtook the competing feelings of cold. Summoning all that was left of him, he raised his spade and delivered the final blow. The problem was that the final blow hit the wrong target. In the dark, in the frigid temperatures, he lost sense of some of his exposed foot. The blow meant for the root ball ended up crashing through his toes.

The man with the beers passed out.

As the icy hands of nature's oldest season gathered upon his neck, an unexpected warmth fell on the face of the man with the beers and helped him regain consciousness. The warmth was an unnatural sensation around such cold. It made him wonder how long he had been unconscious or whether he was gone for good.

"Upon feeling it, that warmth I mean, I reached to heaven and became a believer. Funny, I had been an atheist through the entire foxhole period until drifting off. It was only when I thought I saw evidence of the savior that I embraced it, that I was ready to be born again. But just before that happened, I realized something," the man with the beers said.

"What's that?" Cameron asked.

"Death is a drunk man," the man with the beers said.

It turns out this celestial warmth fountained not from the horn of archangel Gabriel, but from the penis head of Ivan Slitzenokov. A moment later, the man with the beers was an atheist again.

"He saved me because of his own stupidity," the man with the beers said. "That's how humans have always been. We're always falling into holes and finding other people that fall into ones close by that can help us climb out of them."

Back at the hole, Ivan Slitzenokov hoisted the man with the beers onto one shoulder and began to walk back towards the tower. This was met with reluctance by the person he was carrying. That reaction brought him momentary pause.

"Fine," Ivan Slitzenokov said to the man with the beers.

Then he walked back and finished the last of the job on the shrub.

"What happened to your foot?" Cameron asked.

"A toll paid to the tundra," the man with the beers said.

"And the rest of it?" Cameron asked.

"Here, you want to see?" the man with the beers said as he grabbed his left foot and wrenched it forward. He was wearing a chewed-up pair of white Reebok sneakers. "Just kidding," the man with the beers said laughing. "After it happened, Ivan Slitzenokov, drunk as he was, threw me in the car and drove two hours to the nearest hospital. I've since walked with a limp. It's no big deal, really. And when it hurts, I have some things to take to make it feel better. Doc's orders, you know?" he laughed a bit nervously as he shook what must have been a pill case in his pocket. "Though I do have to admit, this clutch on the car is more of an annoyance than I thought it'd be with my leg. My past few cars have been automatics, so I didn't even realize that would be the case."

"Where is it now?" Cameron asked. "The shrub, I mean."

"Since I lost my foot, Ivan Slitzenokov told me to hold onto it. So, I planted it in the yard and it grew into a pretty sturdy hedge. Still there to this day, though it may be floundering a little as of late due to poor care," the man with the beers said. "But anyways. I'm going to jet. You need a ride home?" the man with the beers said.

As enticing as this was, Cameron wasn't willing to drive with a drunk person who had half of their foot missing and couldn't drive stick. So, he declined the offer and exited the Dodge Dart.

"Don't get so hung up on yourself, kid. Make good friends. That's more important. For me, it was most important," the man with the beers said with a smile.

Then he drove off with a swerve.

9

A Bicked Head and a Bowl Cut

Cameron went onto the beach and brought his body down to the sand so he was laying prostrate towards the water. The embrace of the sand on his skin felt good. Its odd combination of cool warmth reminded him of the embrace of a woman. For him, it had been too long.

He stretched his lower back so the stabilizing muscles around his lower spine clamped his vertebrae from all sides. Long ago, he'd read about how such a stretch created an intimacy between Muslims and Yogis and their respective divines. Until now, he hadn't put the pose to use. He only knew of it. And knowing is different than *knowing*. Now, though, it was starting to make sense. For there was something truly satisfying in saluting that retreating ball of fire sinking beneath the horizon.

It would have been nice to share the scene with someone. That type of yearning seemed to pop up all too often as of late. Still, if alone was what he had to be, the beach was a good place for it. He looked at the shoreline. The lack of evidence of the day's activity brought on a simultaneous calm and a pressing anxiety for Cameron. On the one side, it showed how quickly nature could flush out what humanity left behind. On the other side, it showed how fast the past could disappear.

The dry roar of two unhealthy engines abruptly sounded. Both automobiles, one a generic silver sedan and the other a beaten-up black pickup, were packed beyond capacity with scores of people and beach items. The doors opened, and a parade of people, young and old, piled out carrying toys, towels, fishing rods, cooking utensils and what could have been everything else in the world. A group of young men jumped down from the back of the flatbed and kicked a ball amongst themselves. The adults headed up the rear in synchronized fashion with blankets and beach umbrellas. The men wore grass-stained thrift-shop jeans ripped at the knees. Their boots had laces dried by concrete. The women all wore beach dresses over their bathing suits. The older they were, the less skin they showed. Altogether, they appeared to be Mexican folk.

The band headed down towards the far end of the beach in far too systematic a fashion for this to have been a first-time affair. Setup was done with an almost military competency. Some spread the sheets. Others set up chairs and poked umbrellas in the sand. Others filled the grill with charcoal and unpacked food from the cooler. They had the process of utilizing every second of their free time down to a science.

Down the beach, four of these boys, they must have been in their late teens or early twenties, stampeded into the water with barely enough time to take off their shirts. They ran in with long, skinny sticks that looked like javelins. One boy among them carried a big green net instead of the javelin and called out names in Spanish.

Cameron watched them splash around and wrestle each

other into the choppy bay waves with so much happiness on their faces. Their laughs, part pubescent cracks, part developing roars, were infectious. Soon, words turned into action – they attempted a chicken fight. Like most chicken fights, the big strong boys on top enjoyed every second of it, and the small boys that held them up essentially drowned underneath them. A few repetitions of the game, as well as some uncalled-for scratches, were enough for the large boys on top to lose their attention. Impulse then overcame organization. A series of dunkings and wrestling moves impossible to perform on land ensued. This continued until their eyes were swollen from the salt and their muscles grew tired, at which point they returned to their sticks and attended to the business that brought them into the water in the first place.

The water was chest deep where they retrieved their sticks that had floated away during their monkey business. When they had them in hand, they jammed them into the water, making sure they were secure in the sandy-clay bottom. Once stability was established, they attached fishing line to them.

While this went on, Cameron saw a tiny pudgy older woman out of the corner of his eye. Apparently, she was carrying a plate of chicken out to them. Given her size, by the time she reached them, only her forehead and her hands holding the plate with the chicken were above water. Those tending their sticks left their posts to take what she brought them. They showed no signs of concerns for her well-being. Instead, they took the chicken and tied it to the fishing line. Then they tossed it out into the water.

Cameron had seen this version of crabbing. Rather than doing it from the dock, they got in the water, feet fully exposed, and lured the crabs closer and closer, tug by tug, while another person scooped them up with a net when the time was right.

After seeing this, Cameron walked over to where the Mexican folk had set up camp. He quickly noticed that while all the women worked, the lone man, the oldest of the lot, sat relaxed atop a cooler on the outskirts of what was fast becoming kitchen chaos. This El Jefe on the cooler wore ironed slacks and a wife-beater. The latter barely covered a quarter of his stomach. In his mouth was a cigar. On his head was a mesh hat. Patches of whiskers from a few days back covered his face.

El Jefe on the cooler split his attention between watching the kids in the water and watching the three women cooking, chopping vegetables, building sandcastles and setting up sternos. They went from pot to pot as if they were drumming, except this set of drums spat out hot salty water instead of beats. To Cameron's amusement, the dog Lionheart was also there, circling the blanket like a shark for the next piece of food to hit the ground.

In the middle of the blanket, a baby lay in a little screened-in tent. From what Cameron could see, for his line of vision was limited by a hanging zippered door drape, he lay fast asleep on a bed of pillows. He got a little better view when one of the women was spit on by boiling water and cussed everyone out mercifully in random succession. When the woman regained her composure, she went over to the baby's tent and gave the sign of the cross. The same gesture was followed by the other women when they cut themselves a little chopping or got into an argument that escalated out of control.

The youngest of the three women was thirty or so. She had almond skin with dark penetrating eyes and long untamed black hair. The sundress she wore was wet but stayed sandy brown. Just a moment of eavesdropping on the conversation between her and the two other women made it clear that she was equal part sass and smarts. These qualities were on display when she was being bossed around by her two women-elders. She was obedient in Spanish, seemingly the only language the older two women understood, and vengeful in English, cussing them in ways that would make a sailor proud.

Thankfully, the growing tension was broken when the boy who brought the green net into the water brought back a bucket loaded with crabs. All of their scratching and clawing made Cameron confident they knew their fate.

"Do you want to try some when it's ready?" the woman with the sandy-brown sundress asked Cameron.

"What are you having?" Cameron asked.

"Crab bake. Nothing fancy," she said.

"That would be great, thank you," Cameron said. "You are too kind."

The woman in the sandy-brown sundress translated the order to her older female cohorts. Their movements were precise, almost scientific, in response. They weaved back and forth between the boiled pots now beginning to bubble.

With a pair of large metal tongs, the woman in the sandy-brown sundress hovered above the hydrothermal vent that was the crab pot and pulled out a boiled blue claw. Cameron saw the petrified look on the little crustacean's face. The brutal nature of the process that produced that face never ceased to disturb him. All that burning, drowning, and reddening all over, it was pain unimaginable. And for what? The sole enjoyment and engorgement of a few privileged organisms lucky enough to be a few higher links up on the food chain. It just didn't seem right.

CRACK! The shell split in two. The woman in the sandy-brown sundress snapped the crab in half and drained the bodily juices onto the sand where Lionheart licked them up. In seconds, the sea bug went from whole to half, from half to red ash, from nothingness to eventually dog shit. Each crab offered three pieces of meat, one from each claw and one from the chest cavity. Claws went first. The woman's technique was skillful. She grabbed out the meat and stored it in between her fingertips. Then she pried open the chest and took what remained inside the abdomen.

"Seems like a lot of work, all that cracking and peeling, since cangrejo es mas o menos," Cameron said. He was pleased with himself that he remembered the word "crabs" and the phrase "so-so" from all of those years of grade-school Spanish.

At this, the oldest woman grabbed a paring knife and started walking towards Cameron. It took until she was within a few feet of him to realize that her actions were in jest. "You like what you like, right!" She smiled at him with her big brown teeth. Then she said, "but you must try." Cameron was relieved, yet at the same time still distressed by the fact that everyone else seemed relieved she was kidding, too.

The woman with the sandy-brown sundress explained how passionate her aunt and mother were about their cooking. Because of this, they challenged Cameron to eat with them and afterward still have the audacity to say "cangrejo es mas o menos."

Never one to turn down a meal, Cameron agreed to stay and eat.

"Good...then earn your keep...go help them out there," the oldest woman said, and the woman with the sandy-brown sundress translated. She nudged her face towards the water where they were crabbing.

"I don't crab with my toes," Cameron said.

"Para prosperar, tienes que tener algo invertido," said El Jefe on the cooler.

"To thrive you must have something invested," the woman

in the sandy-brown sundress translated, only paying half attention to the conversation as she was being handed more crabs to pot from the other older woman than she could handle. This lack of concentration got the better of the woman with the sandy-brown sundress, causing a crab to escape and a scramble to ensue. The crab crawled for its life across the beach. The woman in the sandy-brown sundress darted after it to avoid her own type of scolding from her elders. It didn't last long before she caught up to it. When she did, the crab proudly put out its pincers, as if to say 'en garde' in one final attempt to fend off an unconquerable foe. At least in terms of the swiftness of the execution, the crustacean's courage paid off. The woman with the sandy-brown sundress's moccasins crushed its chest and appropriately leaked out the dead men inside.

This additional measure did little to convince Cameron of the righteousness of his choice to go in the water and catch more crabs for slaughter. But what the hell, Cameron thought to himself. Such principles could be postponed until after a free meal. So, he took off his shirt and readied himself to join the other crabbers and catch some dinner.

In the meantime, a few of the younger children had grabbed some random clothes that were scattered in the sand and made two soccer goals. During this process, they also grabbed Cameron's shirt, which he regretted taking off as soon as he did so because his pasty white chest amongst all that tan skin easily got the kids' attention. They started calling him milk-man and challenging him to join their game. In response to their provocations, he charged them, stole the ball and tried to show off, purposely mocking himself by poor foot-juggling. 'Milk-man! Milk-man!' they yelled in amusement.

At first, the game was disorganized. It was your classic tackle-the-person-with-the-ball chaos that exists in every schoolyard. The talented formed alliances and agreed to crush the unskilled. Then the game changed. Goals were assembled on opposite sides of the field. The two worst of the lot were thrown in goal. Shots starting firing in their direction before they were even between their "posts."

"Boota! Boota! Where are you going! Necessitas catch your meal. Eat what you kill, eat what you kill! No freeloaders," the oldest woman said, again waving that paring knife of hers. "We have enough of those around here."

A loud whistle blew. When it did, all the boys turned and stood at attention. Inside that dust devil of kicking feet, it was good to hear a call to organization. Cameron tracked the sound to the mouth of El Jefe on the cooler.

"Configurar equipos," El Jefe on the cooler said as he divided them up, using his finger to direct each person to the team they should join. He came to Cameron last. He looked at his wife who seemed adamant about him helping to get some crabs. "Cállate ancianas. Juegas con los chicos. Les gusta Milkman. Eso es lo más importante. Se queda." And with those brief words, there was law in the land. The milkman would stay to entertain the little ones.

A few seconds of watching the way they handled the ball was all it took for Cameron to realize he was outclassed by the kids. To compensate for lack of skill, he summoned his strength. This backfired, as the kids fed off his slide-tackles and his pushing until they eventually brought him to the ground. All of this was done to the tune of the adults' hysterical laughter.

The crabbers still in the bay saw the commotion and couldn't resist taking part. After dropping off their nets and buckets full of fresh caught crabs, the four of them rushed to the field. Again, El Jefe on the cooler ordered each newcomer to a team. The woman with the sandy-brown sundress participated, too. Not long after doing so, she had the ball, and Cameron went to guard her. When he did, she juked one way and then the next and then put the ball between his legs. In dribbling past him, she came before the late-teen-young-twenty-year-old with a bicked head. Her tricks were far less successful against him. With a combination of minimal effort and what appeared to be a brotherly elbow, the late-teen-early-twenty-year-old with a bicked head stole the ball. When she saw a little boy nearby who was laughing at how she was just schooled, she grabbed him and tickled him into submission. Then she walked off the field.

Back to the late-teen-early-twenty-year-old with the bicked head who stole the ball from the women with the sandy-brown sundress. Man, could he dribble. Even in thick sand, he went side to side with unmatched grace and skill. Handles like his belonged in a stadium guarded by walls and ticket prices, not available for free at a sandy beach barbeque. Whenever he passed the ball, Cameron got upset. It was like a magician laying down his wand.

On the side of the field opposite the water was a migratory bird area. It was zoned off by a red sand fence made of panels of cheap plywood strips and sharp metal wire. Since entry was prohibited into the area, it made for a logical and inevitable field boundary. It also was where the ball had just been kicked and where two of the oldest players on the field set out to retrieve it. One player was the bicked-headed-magician. The other was a young gentleman with a bowl cut and a headband. Neither of the two wore shirts. As cumulonimbus clouds signify a coming storm, their style of play was an omen of a coming altercation.

In pursuit of that round, plastic piece of glory, the bicked-headed-magician and the young gentleman with a bowl cut barreled right through the plywood panels. Amidst the wreckage and the shadows supplied by the migratory bird fence, it was hard to tell one from the other. Instead, their bodies became an entangled silhouette. That imagery of unity, however, was not a harbinger of peace. Undeterred and rather motivated by the destruction, they started going at each other, less with fists and more with wrestling moves and headlocks. Though the intensity was equivalent to a street fight, barriers were maintained. Neither crossed it, though they came close, and as a result, nobody bothered to break it up. The carefree attitude of the onlookers suggested that these events occurred with some frequency.

Ultimately, the scuffle only ended due to a cheap shot. When the bicked-headed magician had the upper-hand in a grapple, he used that leverage to pull the hair band of his opponent over his eyes. Temporary blindness ensued. This was followed by a violent takedown, the result of which was the bicked-headed magician retaking possession of the ball. Down but not defeated, the young gentlemen with a bowl cut got up quickly and darted across the field to fetch back what he had lost.

But it was too late. Down on the other side of the field, a pass was made by the bicked-headed magician. The receiver of the pass returned the ball back so quickly one had to double-take to make sure there was ever a change of possession. A man amongst boys, the bicked-headed-magician dodged one player with a juke and then put it through another's legs, a technique he either authored or developed from the sister he earlier stole the ball from. The second he had the right amount of space, he shot a diagonal missile across the goal with the inside corner of his foot.

The shot was more than a shot. It was an echo of memory, a storyline that started with a toddler kicking pebbles in his driveway, parleyed to a youngster pelting soccer balls into spare tires at the schoolyard, and evolved into a neighborhood kid dominating the youth leagues to become what he was now...a bicked-headed magician wielding his foot like a wand.

Each side screamed. The team who shot it celebrated a goal. The other side voiced equally loud notice of disagreement, claiming the shot missed high and wide right. For about a minute, everyone continued to scream. Everyone also continued not to listen. Then, little by little, those with less investment in the outcome went over to the blanket where the crabs were cooking, more interested in filling their stomachs than in being weighed down by the laurels of victory.

Soon, only two people remained on the field: the bicked-headed-magician and the young gentlemen with the bowl cut. They stayed screaming at one another for some time. It was hard to know precisely how long because their yells were quickly muted by conversation back at the blanket.

Cameron followed everyone else in that direction. Initially, he found himself gravitating towards El Jefe on the cooler. When he got over there, he saw the mosquito tent where the baby was sleeping unzip from the inside. A man came out with a rolled up freshly soiled diaper. After a quick juggle, he squared up for a jump-shot into a black garbage bag. It missed. The diaper unrolled. A steamy liquid Gerber Baby shit came into view.

When he shook his head in frustration and went to rebound the diaper, he caught his first glance of Cameron.

"PRIMOS!" he shouted ecstatically.

Cameron shook his hand, and they exchanged happy hellos. Normally, there would be a reluctance to shake hands with someone just juggling shit, but their friendship had been baptized earlier with concrete. He knew this man. He was the Latino from the contractor's construction crew. He mustn't have noticed him earlier since he was laying in the tent with the baby.

"Why weren't you out there?" Cameron asked him. He was referring to the soccer game.

"I'm beat from work, man. You saw what we did today. It got worse when you left. Those guys would argue over whether the sun sets, man," the Latino man from the contractor's construction crew said.

"Well, at least you didn't have to travel far to get here," Cameron said.

"Yeah, not bad. Don't think they just came down here out of convenience for me, though. It's as close or closer for everyone, the two morons included." Then he pointed his head in the direction of the bicked-headed magician and the young gentleman with a bowl cut.

Cameron's eyes also turned to them. It appeared the commotion was concluding. Both were lying in the sand on their backsides. Almost in unison, their stomachs rose up and down like beach balls being blown up and then deflated. "Based on that behavior, you'd never think they'd be good businessmen," the Latino man from the contractor's construction crew said.

"Oh yeah? What do they do?" Cameron said.

"They have an ice cream truck," the Latino from the contractor's construction crew said.

Cameron turned to look at the two of them again. Could it be? Could he have been so imperceptive? True, he'd been transfixed by their feet, so his eyes were drawn away from their faces. They were also shirtless, so the all-white uniform wouldn't have stood out. On second thought, nah, it couldn't be them. They were missing their most defining trait: the two-foot long pony tails. A quick observation of a bicked-head and a bowl cut made him confident that a weird coincidence was simply at play. These were not the Pacos.

"They've been at it all day," said the Latino from the contractor's construction crew. "I can't really blame one over the other. One of them was asleep in the ice cream truck when they were getting lunch today, and when he woke up, his pony tail was cut off. Later in the day, there was apparently retaliation."

"What caused the first one to start the cutting?" Cameron asked.

"It was over some girl, I think. When isn't it, you know? She's actually one of the lifeguards down here, so you may have seen her around. Tough to miss, if you know what I mean. They always give her free ice cream when she's down here. My boss met her on the beach this morning when he was doing his tai chi, and she mentioned she was single again. I let them know as soon as I heard because they never stop talking about her. After they heard, I guess they both tried to make the other one look uglier before the other one could ask her out. Ha! How else could she choose? They're identical."

"Did either of them ask her out?" Cameron asked. He did his best to conceal a tinge of jealousy.

"Nah. They said that another ice cream man was in their spot, so they'd have to wait until tomorrow...like that had anything to do with it...wimps," the Latino from the contractor's construction crew said as he directed his eyes back to the two of them still lying there.

Eventually, the Latino man from the contractor's construction crew turned from watching the Pacos and went back into the tent. He returned with the baby, which he handed to El Jefe on the cooler. The infant climbed all over the old man's soft beer belly until it found the right fold to nestle into.

"Cerveza para bien occupado," the Latino from the contractor's construction crew said to El Jefe on the cooler.

"Beer put to good use," Cameron said smiling.

"Amen. Now let's put our stomachs to good use," the Latino man from the contractor's construction crew said. "Grab a plate and have some crabs."

Cameron looked at El Jefe on the cooler and waited for his nod of approval. Once granted, he headed to the sternos where everything was arranged buffet-style.

The oldest woman was behind the sternos with tongs in her hands. The tongs held a huge crab that the oldest woman brought over and put down on Cameron's plate.

When the rest of his plate was filled to the brim with sides, Cameron pulled up a bucket to sit by the Latino from the contractor's construction crew, El Jefe on the cooler and Lionheart, who was curled beneath the old man's feet. They ate family style, sharing and dipping into everyone else's dish even though they all basically ate the same thing. Cameron was no exception. The second he sat down, El Jefe on the cooler splashed a big piece of crab meat into his butter cup. Apparently, this was a rite of passage because after he did so, all the children followed suit until Cameron had very little butter left.

El Jefe then ordered Cameron to christen his own plate by doing the same. So, Cameron took some meat from his own crab, dipped it in El Jefe's buttery garlic mix, and ate it.

After doing so, he looked across the blanket at the oldest woman who gave him the crab. She had a claw in her mouth and a tiny leg pasted to her cheek from a splash of too much butter. Cameron wasn't sure if she noticed it or simply liked it there. Regardless, he gave her a seated bow and blew her a kiss.

She caught the kiss and pretended to go for her knife again to stab it. Midway down, she stopped herself and smiled back. Then she nodded back in a way that only wise people can do, where they say 'I told you so' without actually saying it.

The woman with the sandy-brown sundress walked over from next to the oldest woman and sat on the lap of the Latino man from the contractor's construction crew.

"I hope you know she's kidding with all the knife stuff," she told Cameron.

"I like a tough woman," Cameron said as he flirtatiously waved back at the old woman.

"Is your girlfriend tough?" the woman with the sandy-brown sundress asked.

"I don't have one," Cameron replied.

"Good for you, kid. Pardon her for being nosy. We were just talking when you were playing with the kids that you'd be a good match for her sister," said the Latino from the contractor's construction crew.

"She's a little smarter than me. A little less pretty," the woman with the sandy-brown sundress said.

"What does she do?" Cameron asked.

"She's a lawyer. We're both lawyers," said the woman with the sandy-brown sundress.

"So, her sister is a lawyer. She is a lawyer, which she said even though nobody asked, and I work construction, as you already know. We're all sharing here. So, what is it that you do?" The Latino from the contractor's construction crew asked.

Cameron paused before saying, "As I said to your boss earlier, I'm trying to figure it out."

El Jefe on the cooler wiped his mouth with his shirt sleeve and blew his nose into the hanky hanging from his neck. Unlike the petty issues of puppy love, this was a topic worthy of his contribution. So, he mumbled a few things in Spanish as he petted Lionheart beside him.

"You will. You will figure it out," El Jefe said via translation by the Latino from the contractor's construction crew.

"How do you know?" Cameron asked.

"Because somewhere inside of you, it's already been figured out. Otherwise you wouldn't be the fine young man I'm looking at today. You just need to give life some time to knock the dust away so whatever it is reveals itself," El Jefe said via translation by the Latino from the contractor's construction crew.

"So, it isn't a matter of discovering, it's a matter of unearthing?" Cameron asked.

"Precisely, Mooncalf. Precisely," El Jefe said in his own words, without translation, as he patted Cameron on the shoulder.

"Mooncalf? What does that mean?" Cameron asked.

"It means you're foolish," the Latino from the contractor's construction crew said.

"Gee, thanks," Cameron said.

"I didn't say that it meant *fool*. I said it meant *foolish*," said the Latino from the contractor's construction crew.

"We're all mooncalfs, my son," El Jefe said in English without translation. "That's what makes the world beautiful."

"Even you?" Cameron asked.

"Especially me," El Jefe said in English, smiling.

10

Friendly Fire

When the Mexican folks pulled away with the sun, Cameron scanned his body. His feet were nicked from beach soccer. Up at his knees, scabs were forming from earlier work with the contractor. Slippery from crab guts, his hands were primed for their next meal. To his surprise, and subsequent pleasure, all of this was evidence of a day truly lived. This made him proud. It made him want to do more of this.

It also made his feet sore. So, he wanted his shoes back.

Cameron passed the house where the little boy with the heart-shaped head lived. A pile of leaves was in the street. Even though the pile was smaller now than it had been in the morning, in all probability, they still belonged to the man with starched khakis. This fact was further confirmed when Cameron realized part of that pile had been concealed from his vision by a familiar parked car, a red Dodge Dart What first caught his attention about the leaves surrounding the Dodge Dart was that they were wet even though it hadn't rained. The culprit must have been that obnoxious sprinkler from before that burned his feet.

The Dart being there was certainly odd. Equally if not more odd, though, was that the hedges separating the lawns were not separating the lawns anymore. Instead, they were rolled up in plastic fish netting and piled on the curb in front of the Dodge Dart.

When Cameron went to the front left-side front of the car, he noticed a dent in the lower bumper. There was also a broken headlight on the same side. These two observations caused him to reexamine his surroundings to try and figure out what happened. Behind him, he found some answers. The corner post of the cyclone fence that divided the two yards, which was now much more visible than before because of the excavated hedges, was tilted back on a forty-five-degree angle. There must have been a heavy impact, because the concrete that secured the corner post into the ground was unearthed. A pair of muddy tire tracks that led up to the corner post confirmed the cause of the disturbance. Still, even with all the evidence pointing toward a recent commotion, at present, all was quiet. It took a faint whimper coming from underneath the vehicle to disrupt that silence.

It was Lionheart.

When Cameron realized this, he crawled underneath the car to tend to the Rhodesian. Once face to face with the dog, Cameron was assured of the worst. Lionheart's spine was wrapped around the cold metal interior frame of the Dart. The end, therefore, was near. And Cameron was not the only living thing under the car who knew it. Inexperienced with similar types of situations, Cameron offered his support the only way that he knew how. He started to rub that infamous tuft of hair that ran across Lionheart's spine. Back and forth, back and forth went his hands, applying just enough pressure to convey emotional support without inducing any physical discomfort.

It was not long until the dog drifted off, then briefly came back, and then drifted off for the last time. Cameron couldn't help but wonder if that interim doze between life and death had shown the dog the greatest secret of them all. That thought captured him for a long while. Eventually, though, duty called. The Dodge Dart was parked in front of the little boy with the heart-shaped head's house. Neither the little boy with the heart-shaped head nor the other boys who would be with him needed to see what Cameron was witnessing. So, in the spirit of letting the children retain their youth for a little while longer, Cameron dragged Lionheart out from under the car and into his arms.

Then he just kind of started walking.

11

Pass the Potatoes

At some point in his wandering, Cameron made his way back down by the canal boat launch. It came as no surprise to him that he was subconsciously directed this way. The path he chose was as close to nature and as far away from houses as he could get in his given location. That sort of thing seems to attract a person when they have just experienced death. That being said, if instinct set his course, what drew him to his destination thereafter were his eyes. Catching their attention was a tiny flickering light in the distance. Cameron followed the flicker. He followed it until he came to a patch of reeds bordering the little side road leading down to the canal boat launch. From there, Cameron could see that the light came from a streetlight that overhung a wooden booth cattycornered between where the boat launch began, and the parking lot stopped – it was the dockmaster's dwelling.

Outside, a man sat on a stool. As soon as the man on the stool saw the dog hanging limp in Cameron's arms, he went over to offer his help.

"Oh, Lionheart," the dockmaster said with a sigh. "What happened?"

"I heard him crying underneath a car," Cameron said. "Before I could get him out…"

"What a shame. That dog's loved around here more than most people. It's so sad to think that some idiot with his car could take away so much joy from a neighborhood. Who was it?" the dockmaster asked.

"I don't know. It was dark," Cameron said. "What should I do with him?" After Cameron said this, he laid the dog down next to them.

"I'm not sure. But while we think about it, let me grab my guitar and pay the animal my respects. Me and him had a lot of good times through the years out here," said the dockmaster. As he said this, he went back inside his little boat shack. An acoustic guitar was in his hand when he came back.

The music that emitted from his instrument provided the conversation that words could not.

"I've never heard someone pluck a six-string like that before. Do you play professionally?" Cameron asked.

The dockmaster smiled. "Not anymore. Now, it's just a good way to pass the time out here while I earn some extra cash.

"Why'd you stop?" Cameron asked.

"You get to a point in your life as a musician when your skills improve and demand for them diminishes. The truth is that no matter how good you are, most people just want to hear you bang on a few chords and make noise," the dockmaster said.

"I'm sorry to hear that," Cameron said.

"It's sad. There is so much hollowness these days," the dockmaster continued. While he spoke, he kept looking at Lionheart. By the way he was muttering, Cameron wondered whether he remembered that there was another person sitting next to him. Nevertheless, he allowed the dockmaster's stream of consciousness to continue without interruption: "Everyone is stuck to their phones. That's one of the big problems. If an explanation is beyond a tweet or a text message, nobody's interested. That same lack of complexity shows in the music."

"I guess it's a tough time to be an artist?" Cameron said.

"It's always a tough time to be an artist," the dockmaster said. "And look, I know good art has always been attacked – that's part of what makes it good art. But it's happening now more than ever, especially at the institutional level. I mean, god forbid you tell people today that you're interested in art when they ask you what you want to do with your life. People seem to think that's an invitation to tell you how much of a mistake you're making. Funny thing, art is. The people who make it, well, they have guts. The people who fail, though, they're just idiots who should've gotten a real job. That never made sense to me. Common sense dictates that art is developed as much by the geniuses as it is by the failures. Yet to strive to make a living doing something so profound is subject to so much social ridicule. Despite all they do for us, one can scoff any time they want at the artist. God forbid, though, I scoff at an accountant. We have to applaud the foresight they have for living so far from the edge. Fuck them. FUCK THEM! I told an accountant when I was younger that I was thinking of becoming an English Professor. She replied by saying, 'For what?' I said I was interested in writing books. She said 'Why? You know nobody will read them except your students because they're forced to?' You know what I told her? I told her that the world would be a better place if people embraced the introspection of the artist. We owe them the grey area of our existence."

"How did she respond?" Cameron asked.

"She told me to pass the potatoes," the dockmaster said.

"I think everyone just has what they care about, and when it doesn't match up with what you care about, it creates frustration," Cameron said. "What that thing is that they care about doesn't make them better or worse, it just makes them different. And unless you're willing to put the time into figuring out that what that thing truly is, it may be unfair to prejudge a person. Who knows, maybe in the long run, it will end up being you, not them, who needs to open up. Be like the boats you're watching man, just go with the flow."

"Easier said than done," said the dockmaster.

"And speaking of boats, what are those kayaks used for over there?" Cameron asked.

Over by the wooded lot, there was a little meandering path made of burnt grass and compacted clay that led to a boat rack. The narrow strip of land had no particular logic to it. In some areas, it was the most direct, most convenient, easiest route. In other places, it went over unnecessary elevations and climbed over sharp rocks even when softer footing was available. It formed because it formed, and that was that. People followed it because, well, that's what people do.

"The kayaks and canoes on the rack are for people with the big boats. When they anchor offshore, they use them to ferry goods from the boat to the beach. This includes any royalty onboard who wants to be transported from knee-deep water to dry sand," the dockmaster said.

"Do they lock them up or anything?" Cameron asked.

"Nah, they don't have to. It's part of my job to keep an eye on them. During the season, there's a dockmaster at every public boat launch on the bay," the dockmaster said.

"Would you mind if I took one out tonight? I'd like to paddle around the canal a bit," Cameron asked.

"Fuck it, dude. I'll go with you. I'm actually required to patrol the canal a few times a night to keep an eye on things anyways. I don't think paddling around as opposed to my usual stroll would compromise that responsibility. We'll take the kayaks. I have mine expertly tied up right here ready to go. There's a shitty one that nobody uses behind the racks over there. We lend it to people who don't have a boat and just want to screw around on the bay. You can't miss it. It's under the blue tarp between two bushes at the edge of the tree line. I'll be waiting here ready with the paddles. I have two sets right in the office here. Bring the tarp back, too. We can wrap the dog up in it," the dockmaster said.

"And then what are we going to do with him?" Cameron asked.

"I'll make sure the dog gets what he deserves. And since I liked this dog more than most people, rest assured he's in good hands. Now go," the dockmaster said.

Cameron made his way on the path towards the boat rack. When he got there, he looked around at the kayaks and canoes. The good ones were elevated, stacked above everyday moisture that could attack their bows. The bad ones were less fortunate. They were slid underneath the rack every which way like a tampered pack of sardines.

Something stirred behind the boats on the other side of the rack. Initially, Cameron paid no attention to it. Instead, he kept his focus on finding the kayak, which he soon located sandwiched in between the two bushes where the dockmaster said it would be. A blue tarp covered half of it, making it seem like someone reconsidered what they were doing and decided not to finish the job.

Cameron ripped the tarp off the kayak and got a full look at the boat he'd soon board. It was a tawny colored structure made of hard plastic composite. In earlier days, it doubtless shined a banana yellow. The years, though, had dulled its image, giving it its fair share of dints and dents. What it kept was its character, and, more importantly, its functionality. For these reasons, Cameron was fast growing fond of the old boat.

So, he drained the watery residue from the kayak, threw the rolled-up tarp in a compartment and hoisted it over his head. Then he began to make his way back to the dockmaster. As he did so, that same strange noise from before resonated from behind the boat rack. This time, curiosity convinced him to follow it.

What he found was two people partially dressed, each enveloped in the other's arms. More specifically, the girl was wrapped around the boy's legs. Her spaghetti straps were unclipped and drawn down to her waist, providing her breasts with a temporary reprieve from their standard garments of oppression that had bounded her since their first day. Sometimes, the partners breathed in unison. Other times, it was a duet-like a jazz jam, with one side soloing and the other offering a baseline until their turn ended. When the man was featured, Cameron observed him thrust into the woman differently than he'd ever seen or done himself – lovingly, genuinely – in pursuit of a purpose beyond lust. Clearly, this was a dance they'd done before.

But who were they? He owed the answer to a creeping full moon and a climax.

The thrusts picked up to a rapid rate before culminating in a mutual moan. When this happened, her neck shot high into the air, and her mane swooshed back carrying a familiar scent of summer flowers. In certain spots, her elevated position allowed her figure to shine in the moonlight. When it did, Cameron recognized the bottom portion of a perfectly S-shaped lower back. On that lower-back was a tattoo of a Viking ship in stormy seas with a siren at the bow.

The man who held her was tall and blond and muscular. Down the visible side of his stomach were a few recently patched-up scars.

Cameron stared at them a second more. Then he gave them back their privacy.

Cameron found the dockmaster floating right beneath his little dwelling in the area where water met the end of the boat ramp. One of his arms held the side of the dock. The other was extended towards Cameron with a paddle in hand. Despite the darkness, Cameron could not help but notice the dockmaster's kayak was pink and polka-dotted.

"Nice boat," Cameron said as he brought the kayak down from his shoulders, hopped into the water and grabbed the paddle that was being offered. "You couldn't have spared me that one?"

"I would've, but it's a recent gift. I needed to captain its first voyage," the dockmaster grinned.

"Fair enough," Cameron said, adjusting his balance in the boat.

"Few things are fair enough, my young friend," said the dockmaster. "For it is 'Fortune, not wisdom, that rules lives.'"

12

Tree of Knowledge

Before long, they were off into the canal, matching each other stroke for stroke. It only took about fifty yards for the dockmaster to fall behind. It probably took another fifty yards for Cameron to realize as much. When he did so, he slowed his kayak. What happened by the boat rack returned to his mind. Indifference was his initial reaction to the memory, but that was just because it was a defense mechanism. Truth be told, he was crushed by what he saw. And since the emotional toll was created entirely from a brief conversation he'd had with a stranger on a dock, the whole thing made him feel stupid – really stupid. Suddenly, though, that didn't seem to matter. More important than feeling smart was having the ability to feel. Yes, Cameron wanted to feel. He wanted his humanity delivered back to him.

These conclusions made his mind go quiet for the first time in a long while. This allowed for other sensations to fill the void. The cool air of the bay breeze was one of these things. Cameron first felt it on the rivets between his nose and mouth.

He next felt it during its gentle passing over his ears and the top of his head.

Underneath the boat, the current performed similar functions on his feet. With each additional rock back and forth, the water felt less like water and more like an extension of his bloodstream. All of this connectedness around him at once, all of it working together, was such a comfort. Knowing he was as much the wind and the water as he was himself made being himself so much easier, so much less scary.

Still, all of this was a bit much for him. So, he cried.

He cried from a deprivation of human touch, and weekends wasted in worry, and all the memories that could have been with better management of his issues. After that, he cried for abandoning his one true belief, which was that life was the ultimate gift and therefore life deserved to be treated as such. Lastly, he cried out of relief, relief that, little by little, everything would be okay. And when it wasn't, that everything would eventually be okay again sometime soon after that.

He circled that area of the canal for who knows how long. In fact, maybe he wasn't even circling. Straight lines can be circles in the dark. Anything can be anything in the dark.

With that, Cameron paddled on back down the canal. Trees stood still. Again, the sea was glass. Cameron looked at the boats around him. They were positioned down the canal in size order. Only the space for the little ferry boat broke this pattern, as it was empty. When he saw this, he paddled over to the spot and anchored his hand onto the side of the dock. Through the large empty space, he looked out onto the road. A large house across the street from the canal caught his eye. The front door light was on. A man wearing a flat cap and a black suit was on the stoop. Although he stood facing the door, he was not knocking.

An SUV packed with people pulled up to the house. Everyone who got out was dressed in black. Cameron could see them quite clearly because light sensors lit up the whole lawn when they reached the walkway. Two men led the group up the steps. Once there, they embraced the man still standing there. Behind the two men was a middle-aged woman Cameron had never seen before. She had three little boys by the hand. Two of them looked like clones of different sizes. The third boy had no physical resemblance to the other two. Behind them, a very large fat man labored with a woman a quarter of his size on his arm. Rounding up the party was a younger woman with a striking resemblance to the older woman in front of her. The hand of a tall young blond man graced her hip.

With what appeared to be encouragement from the group huddled around him, the old man reached into his slacks pocket and fiddled around for a key. Once he found it, he put it into the door and turned the knob. For a moment after it swung open, he seemed to grow tentative again. Alert to the sudden shock, the two men embraced him on either side and ushered him inside. The rest of the party followed, and before long, the house was alive. When the first lights turned on, Cameron saw that the bay window was adorned with red and white flowers, some of which were in the shape of the cross.

At the sight of this, Cameron decided to push off from the side of the dock and continue paddling back towards the boat ramp. It was no surprise to see the polka-dotted kayak out of the water, leaning against the dockmaster's booth. The dockmaster himself was inside the booth, but his window facing the canal was open. Cameron hollered over to him to ask if he could finish his lap around the back of the cove. The dockmaster waved back through the tiny window facing the canal and told him to take his time.

When Cameron reached the back of the cove, he ran the boat ashore. He did so on the muddy bank right next to the bench where he had sat with the homeless-looking woman earlier that morning. From there, he headed to the tree with his shoes.

Just then, a large light burst through the trees. It came from a tractor idling on the side of the Old Shoaling Road.

"You still need those shoes?" a voice with a mouth full of food yelled from the little tractor. It was the contractor. He was driving the Bobcat. Evidently, he had finally gotten it to work.

"You bet," Cameron said. "How'd you get the Bobcat fixed?"

"It was the funniest thing. A brilliant gal came by after you left, and we struck up a conversation. She said she was watching us for the past few days and hated seeing such a good machine out of commission – used to work on helicopter engines in the military. In about five minutes of her tinkering, the engine was up and running again. The second I heard that engine hum again, I put a job offer on the table. She starts tomorrow," the contractor said.

"That should impact crew dynamics?" Cameron asked.

"It actually worked out well. I needed someone to take Dewayne's spot after he quit today. You'd think a Ph.D. in particle physics would've enjoyed working with concrete. That was my thinking when I hired him a while back. Maybe that tangle with the ice cream man today was just too much for him," the contractor said.

"What are Dewayne's plans moving forward?" Cameron asked.

"The market is a little better now. I'm sure he'll wind up going back to what he used to do," the Contractor said.

"I guess that's good news," Cameron said. "I could use some good news right now."

"Are you referring to Lionheart?" the Contractor asked. "I was just with the gentleman who handles the dock. He told me what happened when he flagged me down to dig a hole."

"Good thing you had your machine," Cameron said.

"He told me you were the one that got him out from under the car. That's a shame. Earlier today, there was a fiasco at the location where the dog was hit. One of my workers dates a relative. He got some of the story on the phone from his girlfriend while it was happening. I'll learn more tomorrow, but I know the two houses belong to a pair of brothers who really got into it bad."

"What about?" Cameron asked.

"Not sure. From what I heard, they had a rocky relationship. I know their mom died a day or so ago. I also know one of them has been battling an opiate addiction, and the other one has his own slew of mental issues. Apparently, he took down all of the hedges on his brother's property without even asking," the contractor said.

"That would have pissed me off, too," Cameron said.

"Yeah, added to that, the rumor is that some infidelity was afoot between the wife and the brother," the contractor said as he pointed the floodlight from his Bobcat up into the branches of the tree above them. "Anyways, which shoe was it?"

"What?" Cameron asked, trying to understand the question.

"I said which shoe was it?" the contractor said.

Cameron looked up into the trees and saw pairs and pairs of shoes.

"Looks like we got ourselves a good old-fashioned shoe tree here. I love shoe trees. I've seen a couple of them out West. I can't believe I didn't notice this in all the days I've driven past it to get to the jobsite. I guess it's because it's a tad off the street... Here, climb in the bucket, and I'll raise you up to find yours."

When Cameron was in the bucket at eye-level with the shoes in the branches, he noticed some familiar footwear. An old pair of brown Clark Loafers was closest to him. When he flicked them so they would spin around like a mobile, Cameron noticed something written inside the tongue of the shoe. The passage stated the following:

"Life is divine Chaos. It's messy, and it's supposed to be that way." JK

THERE WAS ALSO A PAIR OF GIGANTIC LIME GREEN CROCS. INSIDE one of the heels was a drawing in Sharpie marker of two men, a large one and a small one, laughing and eating ice cream amongst a flock of seagulls. Despite the difficulties of drawing on the heel of a shoe with a thick marker, it suffered from no lack of intricate detail.

A pair of chewed-up white Reeboks hung next to the Crocs. This tongue read: *"To understand all is to forgive all."*

Other shoes hung from the tree as well, but he didn't bother to read them. The inscriptions were now a covenant between shoe and tree.

So, he grabbed his shoes and started to unwind them from the branch. Suddenly, a startling noise came from higher up in the tree. Fears of facing off against some large bird were short-lived when he saw its cause. Swinging back and forth on a branch were a pair of concrete-stained work boots. Instead of going up to inspect them more carefully, Cameron signaled for the contractor to lower him down.

Back on the ground, neither Cameron nor the contractor had any shoes or boots on.

13

A Secret in the Garden

The next morning, a Caribbean man with a vueltiao was walking down the Old Shoaling Road. When he passed the man with starched khakis' house, he noticed that the lawn was in disorder. Maybe that wasn't fair. It was only in disorder compared to its normal appearance. If it was compared to every other house on the block besides the Caribbean man with the vueltiao's, then it still maintained its aesthetic superiority. This made the Caribbean man with the vueltiao chuckle because he knew how much it bothered the man with starched khakis to be second best at anything.

One additional scan of the lawn was all it took for the Caribbean man with the vueltiao to notice what was different about it. The curb was where he found his answer. Ready for trash pickup, the shrubs that formerly divided the man with starched khakis' lawn from his neighbor were wrapped up and stacked on the street. Next to them on the curb were multiple bags of leaves and a garbage can.

Out of habit, he glanced into the garbage can. It was a

worthwhile venture to do so, as every so often, the man with starched khakis tossed out something valuable. Lucky for the Caribbean man with the vueltiao, this was one of those times. For staring at him, in pieces were the broken remains of Borodino, the ghoulish statue that he so often would light a cigarette and pour whiskey for while socializing with the man with the beers. With those memories in mind, the Caribbean man with the vueltiao could not leave the statue to its current fate. So, he grabbed the pieces of Borodino to take with him.

When he got back to his house, he set Borodino on his stoop. It didn't take more than a minute or two of tinkering to conclude that the statue was beyond repair. Never one to waste, the Caribbean man with the vueltiao fetched his hammer and chisel and began to tap away at it. When the pieces were finally pounded to powder, he swept them up with his hand broom and brought them over to his front gate in a dustpan. The hope was that since the limestone statue contained calcium, a mineral the Caribbean man with the vueltiao's plants needed for good health, his friend and neighbor's most prized possession could be reborn in another form.

And so there, buried beneath blooming flowers, Borodino's remains lay secretly scattered, in dutiful watch over all inhabitants of the Old Shoaling Road.

About the Author

David O'Boyle is a native of Long Island, New York. He earned a Bachelor of Arts in English and in History from the University of Maryland, College Park. After working for a few years in Manhattan as a headhunter he enrolled at City University of New York School of Law (CUNY Law) and obtained his Juris Doctorate.

Mooncalfs is his first novel.